"Miranda, are most men intimidated by your wicked tongue?" Trent asked. "Do they skulk off to a suitable distance after you zing them with those sweet little put-downs?"

"They do if they're gentlemen—a concept probably unfamiliar to you," she snapped, then regretted it. There was just something about Trent that rubbed her the wrong way, and made her say the wrong things.

His laugh surprised her. "You're right about that. Even the word *gentleman* sounds a lot tamer than I ever plan to be."

Miranda didn't need any reminders that tame and Trent were contradictions in terms. His muscular physical presence was proof enough. Too easily he goaded her into being prissy and critical, and he seemed to relish it.

She decided to try a different approach. "Trent, I admit I sometimes act high-handed. But I can't figure out why you keep trying to shock me and make me ill at ease."

"Can't you, Mandy? Can't you tell when somebody wants you to take notice? To look at him as a man? He'll stoop to just about any tactic that will work." His thumb outlined her lower lip. "I'm no different. If I acted polite, acted deferential as you seem to think the hired help should, would you give me anything but a polite response?"

"I—"

"We both know you wouldn't." He tipped her chin up. "So, like an adolescent, I resort to teasing and showing off to get a girl's attention." His eyes had never seemed so blue. "I'm chasing you, Mandy. . . ."

W9-CLA-200

WHAT ARE *LOVESWEPT* ROMANCES?

They are stories of true romance and touching emotion. We believe those two very important ingredients are constants in our highly sensual and very believable stories in the *LOVESWEPT* line. Our goal is to give you, the reader, stories of consistently high quality that may sometimes make you laugh, sometimes make you cry, but are always fresh and creative and contain many delightful surprises within their pages.

Most romance fans read an enormous number of books. Those they truly love, they keep. Others may be traded with friends and soon forgotten. We hope that each *LOVESWEPT* romance will be a treasure—a "keeper." We will always try to publish

LOVE STORIES YOU'LL NEVER FORGET
BY AUTHORS YOU'LL ALWAYS REMEMBER

The Editors

Loveswept ® 498

Linda Jenkins
Too Far to Fall

BANTAM BOOKS
NEW YORK · TORONTO · LONDON · SYDNEY · AUCKLAND

TOO FAR TO FALL

A Bantam Book / October 1991

LOVESWEPT® *and the wave device are registered
trademarks of Bantam Books, a division of
Bantam Doubleday Dell Publishing Group, Inc.
Registered in U.S. Patent
and Trademark Office and elsewhere.*

*All rights reserved.
Copyright © 1991 by Linda Jenkins.
Cover art copyright © 1991 by Ed Tadiello.
No part of this book may be reproduced or transmitted
in any form or by any means, electronic or mechanical,
including photocopying, recording, or by any
information storage and retrieval system, without
permission in writing from the publisher.
For information address: Bantam Books.*

*If you would be interested in receiving protective vinyl
covers for your Loveswept books, please write to this address
for information:*

> Loveswept
> Bantam Books
> P.O. Box 985
> Hicksville, NY 11802

*If you purchased this book without a cover you should
be aware that this book is stolen property. It was re-
ported as "unsold and destroyed" to the publisher and
neither the author nor the publisher has received any
payment for this "stripped book."*

ISBN 0-553-44180-9

Published simultaneously in the United States and Canada

*Bantam Books are published by Bantam Books, a division
of Bantam Doubleday Dell Publishing Group, Inc. Its trademark, consisting of the words "Bantam Books" and the
portrayal of a rooster, is Registered in U.S. Patent and
Trademark Office and in other countries. Marca Registrada.
Bantam Books, 666 Fifth Avenue, New York, New York
10103.*

PRINTED IN THE UNITED STATES OF AMERICA

OPM 0 9 8 7 6 5 4 3 2 1

One

"Couldn't you wait until morning to take a shower? It's after midnight and I was kind of . . . tied up."

Miranda Hart's fingers tightened around the brass knob of her apartment door. *This* was the maintenance man she had phoned only five minutes ago? Leaning against the doorframe, he watched her from beneath half-closed eyelids. Bright red letters blazed out at her from his chest-hugging T-shirt. BE SAFE—SLEEP WITH A MARINE. Ripples of pure female awareness played along her nerve endings and settled in the pit of her stomach.

If this man was safe, so was a powder keg in a forest fire.

Her chin rose a notch. "One of the benefits of living in this high-rent building is supposed to be twenty-four-hour-a-day maintenance service." Struck by how grouchy and out of sorts she sounded, Miranda started to apologize. But the amusement brightening his eyes silenced her.

She swallowed and gripped the knob even tighter. Looking into blue-gray eyes identical in color to her own startled her. It was as though some mystical kinship linked them. She glanced away, confused because she rarely had such fanciful notions. Struggling to recall her original train of thought, Miranda asked, "Or did I misinterpret my lease agreement, Mr. . . . ?"

"Trent," he supplied helpfully, his mouth curving into a grin that was every bit as lazy as his stance. "And, no, you didn't misunderstand the lease."

"Well, then, Mr. Trent," she said, opening the door for him to enter, "I suggest we take care of my problem so you can get back to your rope tricks." At his questioning look, Miranda sighed and wished she had resisted the clever jibe. "You said you were tied up. Tied up . . . rope tricks."

"Oh. Right." His laugh revealed a row of straight, stunningly white teeth. It also spawned laugh lines at the corners of his eyes and carved a groove in his left cheek. "But forget the Mr.," he corrected, ambling past her into the dimly lighted foyer. "Just Trent's enough."

Miranda drew a deep breath and shut the door, finally relinquishing her stranglehold on the damp brass. "Just Trent" didn't fit her picture of a maintenance man. Nor did he act like one. She frowned, annoyed that his appearance and attitude made her uneasy. It wasn't fear, she realized, but a kind of internal warning system that urged caution simply because he was near.

Giving herself a silent scolding, Miranda secured the dead bolt with a decisive flick of her wrist. So what if his beard made him look slightly dangerous, or that he'd boldly assessed her with eyes that seemed to see more than she cared to reveal. She even dismissed the roguish grin as harmless. Oh, she didn't doubt it could captivate a more susceptible woman. But Miranda Hart was immune. In control. "Just Trent" had only come to do a job.

Confidence restored, she whirled around to show him the bathroom where the shower drain needed unclogging. But without waiting for an invitation or directions, he was already sauntering down the narrow hallway toward the master suite as if he made the trip with regularity. His slow, loose-limbed gait suggested that hurry wasn't his favorite word, but somehow he'd managed to get ahead of her while she'd stood motionless, convincing herself that he was harmless. *What nerve!*

She trailed after him, the high heels of her satin and lace mules telegraphing her agitation against the hardwood floor. After calling the emergency maintenance number, she'd hurriedly changed from her robe into more suitable clothes. Why hadn't she put on sneakers or Loafers instead of these ridiculous slippers that made her mince around? She caught up with him only because he paused to study her lighted display cases lining the hallway.

"Fancy yourself a modern-day Noah?" he asked, commenting on her collection of animal pairs.

"No, it's just a hobby." She didn't have an explanation for why she'd started collecting them nearly ten years ago.

"Some hobby. Must be at least a hundred of 'em."

"One hundred twenty-seven, at last count. Not all of them are in here." Why was she wasting time with this?

Putting herself back in charge, she said, "The bathroom's this way." She led him through her bedroom and into the connecting bath. The room was large and luxurious, but Miranda knew at once it wasn't big enough to share with a man like Trent.

He wasn't unusually tall, probably only six or seven inches over her five feet five. His shoulders weren't excessively broad, although at first they appeared to be because the rest of him was so much narrower. Still, he exuded such a tangible maleness that Miranda felt it all the way to her toes. They tingled against the satin of her slippers.

He dropped a tool box on the moss-green bath mat, but rather than concentrating on her sluggish plumbing, he stared at the vivid red silk kimono hanging on a brass hook beside the tub.

Lean brown hands slid over the robe's delicate softness. Silence intensified the faint clicks made by calloused male fingers snagging the material, and Miranda forgot to breathe. He traced the golden dragon on the back, then grasped the lapel and made a fist, rubbing, crushing.

She blinked and shook her head. Had she really seen that or was it only an hallucination? Trent stood with his hands jammed palms outward in the back pockets of almost-colorless jeans. Jeans, she couldn't help observing, that hung so low, she hoped he didn't inhale sharply or the denim might give up its battle to stay on his hips.

"Aren't you afraid of losing your pants?" she blurted out, snapping her mouth shut after she heard herself speak the thought aloud.

"Can't have that," he said, transferring his thumbs to the beltless loops so he could hitch the jeans up a few inches. "I never show my dimple to anyone I've just met."

Miranda choked on a half gasp, half laugh. She, who never made forward remarks, had just admitted she'd been checking out a stranger's backside. Worse yet, she'd been finding its taut contours utterly fascinating. At least she hadn't confessed that too. When Trent didn't turn around, she vowed to keep quiet and keep her eyes trained on neutral territory.

What had gotten into her? Exhaustion, she rationalized, kneading an aching shoulder muscle. That had to be the explanation for her preoccupation with his anatomy.

After conducting a grueling five-day motivation seminar in Denver, she'd flown home late Friday night to spend the entire weekend moving into her new apartment. All the exertion had prompted her to take a long, steamy shower despite the late hour. A decision that had ultimately unleashed this masculine invader in her retreat.

Unobtrusively, Miranda kicked off her frivolous mules and scooted them behind the antique wicker trunk she used as a clothes hamper. That was when she noticed he was barefoot.

Winter was lingering in Kansas City. People had worn wool in today's Easter Parade, the first week in April. "Isn't it too chilly to go without shoes?" *Oh, for heaven's sake*, she thought with increasing self-disgust. *He must wonder why I'm so obsessed with what he's wearing.* She wondered the same thing herself.

"I didn't have to come far." He pushed aside the billowy floral-print shower curtain and flashed her a sly grin. "Lucky for you, huh?"

"Indeed," she agreed crisply, even as some basic

feminine instinct recognized that luck would play no part in her dealings with Trent. Now her imagination was really acting up. She'd probably never see the man again.

She watched him bend over and glare at the faucets. He had the kind of hair Miranda had envied all her life. Thick, tawny brown with gold streaks, it was cropped short around the ears and in back, but spilled in an undisciplined sweep over his tanned forehead. Nothing like her own fine chestnut locks, which required expert cutting and styling.

She reached up to fluff her bangs and smooth back the sides of her sleek new hairdo, then quickly clasped her hands together behind her. It wouldn't do for Trent to get the mistaken impression that she was preening for him. He'd have no way of knowing she never did that sort of thing.

He jiggled the stopper up and down several times. The trapped water gave a loud gurgle, but resisted going down the drain. At this point, Miranda wished she'd just soaked in the tub and left the water standing until the regular maintenance man could repair it tomorrow.

Trent now stood with his arms crossed, looking perplexed as he eyed the fixtures. It wasn't an expression that inspired confidence. Going to bed stiff and sticky seemed increasingly certain to Miranda. "Can you fix it?" she asked, hoping for a miracle.

"I can do a lot of things," he drawled, turning to overwhelm her again with the impact of all that overt masculinity. His smile was so indolent, she'd have sworn it required every bit of his energy. The unabashed gleam in his eyes told her he could sweep a woman away faster than Dorothy's twister, and that he probably had. Lots of times.

Her mouth went dry, and she had to force herself to face him resolutely. Though they were separated by several yards, she had an absurd compulsion to flee.

"Look," she said, using sheer willpower to summon her coolest voice. "I have an early appointment in the morning, and I really need to get some sleep." She'd banish Trent and hope that insomnia would take a night off. "I'll call George tomorrow," she offered, recalling the teddy bear of a man who'd handled all her work requests before she moved into the apartment. "He can take care of it then."

"I didn't say I can't fix it," Trent said, still regarding her with his unnerving grin. "I just like to take my time, do a job right."

He hoisted his tool box and started to advance. All traces of humor vanished abruptly. His darkening eyes captured her gaze, held her immobilized, made it impossible for her to pull in enough air. When he spoke, his voice was so soft, Miranda found herself straining to hear.

"But then, life works like that, doesn't it, Mandy? Some things take a long, long time."

With that cryptic statement, he broke their eye contact and brushed past her, so close that she drew away from the heat of him. She let out a shaky breath, not quite trusting her voice to inform him that she allowed no one except her baby sister to get by with calling her Mandy. But she had to say something, if for no other reason than to affirm that she was still capable of rational thought. "Where are you going?"

Over his shoulder, she could see one brow arch suggestively. "To your bedroom, of course."

"Excuse me," she said, following on his heels. "I must not have heard you correctly."

He had her closet door opened wide before she could stop him. "The trapdoor to your bathtub plumbing is in here, at the back." He dug for a flashlight, dropped to his knees, and crawled out of sight.

For the next few minutes, Miranda paced, listening to a steady stream of pounding, wrenching metal, and cursing. From the commotion, she feared the drain would never function again. At last he materialized, sucking on a scraped knuckle. "All done. You should have clear sailing now."

Surprised and relieved, she smiled. "Thank you. If I . . . I'm sorry if I sounded rude. This weekend has been a hassle, trying to get everything moved, unpacked, and in place."

"No problem," Trent said, matching her smile. "I'm always prepared to rescue a damsel in distress."

He didn't look like any Boy Scout Miranda had ever seen. Nor did he look as though he belonged in her bedroom. He was too observant. She'd seen him checking out her lace-canopied bed. That and the antique porcelain doll contradicted the sophisticated image she aspired to.

"Well, thanks again," she said, an obvious ploy to send him on his way.

He took the cue, though not until he sent her a silent message. *I know you want me out of here, but I'll be back.*

Hallucinating again, she told herself, leading him back to her front door. No maintenance man who valued his job would make the mistake of trifling with a tenant.

She opened the door. He didn't move. "Is there something else?"

"Uh-huh. I like the way you smell."

Before Miranda could find her voice, he was halfway to the elevator. Vexed, she gave the door a healthy shove.

She swore she could hear laughter.

Lady Miranda wasn't the only one who needed sleep. Unlocking the leasing office, Trent smiled at his nickname for the prim woman he'd just left on the fourth floor. He was tired, as he always was after a camping trip. Keeping up with four active boys required heavy-duty stamina. But tonight, curiosity took priority over fatigue.

He hadn't exactly been salivating to see the new tenant, even after George Timmons had told him, "Wait 'til you get a load of this one. She'll really crank you up." He chuckled, slouching in the executive chair. George worried a lot more about Trent's love life, or lack of one, than Trent did.

During the past few weeks he'd been treated to George's explicit descriptions of the "babe" who would be moving into 4-D. So when she phoned earlier and he had a voice to match the face and body he'd been hearing about for a while, he'd decided to answer the call himself. Especially when he'd detected a hint of desperation buried within her almost-arrogant demand that the shower be fixed, and fast.

Because he didn't respond well to demands these days, he'd had a mind to give Ms. Hart a taste of reciprocal arrogance. He had dismissed the idea quickly. Trent was no longer into power games.

She had tried to remain so detached and elegant, but the sweet fragility of her features and the wariness in her eyes betrayed her. In recent months, Trent had learned a lot about reading people, and he suspected that her aloofness masked a vulnerable core. Miranda Hart intrigued him more than anyone or anything in a long time. Which said a lot about the strength of her appeal.

Trent had been caught up in a love affair with life for the past year. Many people and projects had claimed his time and attention. But none so instantly or so intensely as the lady upstairs.

He removed a key ring from the desk and opened the file cabinet, thumbing through folders until he found what he was looking for. After a quick scan of the lease, he scowled at Miranda Hart's application form. Fair-Day Properties ought to require more detailed information of its tenants.

The sheet revealed that Miranda L. Hart was a vice president at Callahan Associates. That could mean anything with such a diversified company. He'd met Sam Callahan, and knew that his company was a familiar name locally as well as nationally. It was into brokerage, accounting, insurance, investments, and consulting, making it impossible for him to guess what Ms. Hart actually did.

He skimmed the rest of the form, nodding when the final item confirmed his assumption that there was no husband in the picture. Leslie Hart, M.D., was to be notified in case of emergency.

"Excellent!" Trent whispered, sounding like one of his youthful charges. The Harts must be related, possibly sisters, but never had there been more unlikely siblings. Regal Miranda had greeted the maintenance man wearing classy clothes and pearl earrings. He had gotten to know the irrepressible Dr. Les through the volunteer work they both did, and everything in her wardrobe came from thrift shops.

Trent dropped the folder back in place and shoved the drawer closed. His initial curiosity had been replaced by a need to know more. Good thing he had all the time in the world to search for answers. He locked the office door, humming while he waited for the elevator. His friend Sean had been so right. If only you'd slow down enough, you'd find life full of unexpected pleasures.

Miranda slammed the last cabinet door shut, exasperated that she couldn't find a single coffee bean. She double-checked the freezer. No Colombian Supremo there either.

So they'd be ready first thing this morning, her grinder and coffee maker had been one of the first things she'd unpacked. How could her efficient inventory system have failed, causing her to run out of something as vital as coffee? Deep in thought, she drummed closely trimmed nails on the white ceramic counter.

She could alter her routine. One of her favorite food shops was now within walking distance. By the time she got ready for work, the store would be open. She'd planned to be at the office extra early, but she could compensate by staying late, a habit she had formed years ago.

After a quick shower, Miranda smoothed on scented body lotion, remembering Trent's comment when he left her apartment last night. "I like the way you smell." Oddly enough, she'd sensed the compliment was straightforward, lacking the subtle suggestiveness of several of his earlier remarks. What would he say if he knew the fragrance was called Miranda, that she had it custom-blended just for her by a chemist? If he were anything like her sister, he'd accuse her of being a hedonist.

She plunked the bottle down with force. Why did she always feel guilty when she indulged herself? Miranda closed her eyes and shook her head. She *shouldn't*! Not after all the times she'd scrimped and counted every penny, doing without not only things she'd wanted, but necessities as well. That was all behind her, she reassured herself, striding to the closet to pull out out one of her stylish suits.

In less than ten minutes, she strode through the building's lobby. Outside, she inhaled deeply, reveling in the promise of spring. This time of year always filled her with hope, put an extra bounce in her walk. Half a block down the street, Miranda couldn't resist slowing at one of the city's countless fountains. The water wouldn't be turned on until the summer, yet she relaxed when she thought of the soothing sight and sound and movement it would make as it pursued a never-ending cycle. After a few moments, she pushed herself to hurry. Waxing poetic over an empty fountain was a frivolouos waste of time.

"Morning, Mandy."

She didn't have to turn around to know who had drawled the soft greeting. "Good morning," she returned with brisk politeness, not stopping. "And it's Miranda, not Mandy."

Out of the corner of her eye she saw Trent draw even, felt his steady, silent appraisal, waited for his response to her correction. It never came.

Instead, he inspected her suit and pumps, then asked, "Where are you headed? Surely you don't go to work this early."

She often did precisely that, but saw no point in telling him. Overtime was probably a foreign concept to someone like Trent. "I couldn't find any coffee so I'm going to Gourmet Grocer."

He stepped in front and turned to face her all in one smooth motion, forcing her to stop or risk a collision. Pale light beamed golden in his hair and reflected off his beard. The acute awareness of him she had felt last night was heightened this morning. He seemed larger, stronger, as if dawn had intensified the already-potent effect he had on her senses. She edged back a couple of steps, needing to distance herself from too much exposed skin and rippling muscle.

Her eyes countermanded her brain's orders. They took a leisurely tour, past sinewy arms, down from the sleeveless yellow T-shirt cropped just below his pectorals, over a flat, tanned stomach, around the damp coils ringing his navel. Lower.

The shorts designer's main goal must have been conservation of material and thread. Electric blue nylon clung with the same determination as the previous night's denim, and the split sides left little to her imagination. It wasn't until Trent extended one leg back to stretch that she stirred enough to drag her gaze up. Right after she'd seen the scars spanning his knee.

Their eyes met, and Miranda realized his lazy lids were dangerously deceptive. Often they hid laughter and mischief; never did that shuttered gaze miss anything. He knew she'd been admiring his body. Knew, also, the moment she had noticed the scars.

Flustered at being caught, she babbled, "You jog for exercise?"

"Nah, not really," he said, stretching the leg again. "On the other hand, I can't resist betting on a sure thing."

"You run because of a wager?" She'd have bet he wouldn't expend his effort to run, period.

"A friend challenged me, and I couldn't turn down the chance to rub his nose in his own superiority." His grin widened. "He says my, uh, choice of recreation doesn't keep me in good enough aerobic condition to run the number of miles that he does every week. Claims I'm in lousy shape."

Miranda ignored the innuendo and resumed walking. She'd never tell him, but his shape looked plenty impressive to her. There it was again. That disturbing physical perception of him as a man. And herself as a woman. She cleared her throat and tried to sound less interested than she really was. "How much will you win if you prove him wrong? Or lose, if you don't?"

"Oh, I won't lose," he assured her with confidence. "But the stakes aren't money. He thinks I'll have to run thirty miles a week with him for the next six months." Trent fell into step alongside her. "Instead, he's going to find himself tagging along with me. On one of my escapades, as he calls them."

Miranda didn't care to pursue the exact nature of his escapades, so she picked up the pace on the outside chance that he'd had enough exercise for one day. No such luck. Unlike her, he wasn't even breathing hard.

"This trip isn't necessary, Mandy. Haven't you

heard of that time-honored custom of borrowing from a neighbor?"

The corners of her mouth twitched at his suggestion. "Since I only moved in, I don't know a neighbor."

"You know one. Me."

Miranda halted again, scanning the buildings on either side of the street. Even the smallest units in this part of town carried hefty price tags. "You live nearby?"

"Uh-huh." He touched her arm lightly, briefly. "Let's go back to my place, and I'll officially welcome you to the neighborhood." As if he expected the sharp look that preceded her refusal, he quickly added, "I'll give you some coffee, and you won't even have to pay it back."

She hesitated, mentally compiling a list of reasons why she shouldn't venture onto his turf. Before she could voice an excuse, Trent steered her in the opposite direction and they were retracing her route. All the way to the door of her building.

"You live *here*, Trent?"

"Here, Mandy. At your beck and call. Anytime. Day . . . or night."

Two

Miranda fumbled for the door handle, but her fingers tangled with Trent's. She jerked her hand back as if he'd given her a shock. In fact, he had. Learning that she and Trent were neighbors, combined with his persistent use of her nickname, was enough to rattle her. However, it was the implied possibilities his voice evoked when he volunteered his services day or night that sparked flashes of heat.

While Trent led her to the elevator, she tried to tell herself it made sense for Fair-Day Properties to provide an apartment for its after-hours maintenance man. But he used a key to access the top floor. Miranda knew the rates increased upward with each floor. By the time the doors whooshed open on the fifth floor, she had come up with an astronomical figure.

Instead of four front doors gracing the hallway like on the other floors, there were only two. Neither was numbered.

"Are you sure you live here?" she asked when Trent ushered her into a huge loft.

"Last time I checked." He turned a complete circle, taking in the panorama of electic clutter. "Yep, I recognize the mess."

Miranda didn't believe for a second that a company would give up so much lucrative rental space to an employee. This many square feet represented a substantial amount of income.

Trent must have read her mind because he shrugged and answered her unasked question. "Hey, if you were close to the owner and he offered you a place like this rent-free, wouldn't you jump at the chance?"

Miranda didn't understand why, but she felt let down that he was the type who'd accept such generosity. Then she reprimanded herself for caring. She'd only come for the coffee, not an assessment of Trent's character. With that mission in mind, she marched past him.

The room, punctuated at intervals by fluted columns, stretched along one side of the building, a space that would normally hold two apartments. The area where they had entered could not technically be termed a foyer, though it did contain an oak coatrack. A scuffed bomber jacket dangled from the top hook, its leather dull and soft from repeated wear. In contrast, a rainbow of small parkas ringed the jacket.

Miranda froze, suddenly feeling as if she had waded into quicksand. She stole a side long peek at Trent who was studying her reaction. She couldn't believe she had wasted even a second fantasizing about a man who had fathered a houseful of little parka wearers.

Dead ahead she spied a bulletin board covered with what had to be children's crayon artwork. Stick figures and crooked houses vied for space with some fairly accurate depictions of mountains and forests. Her gaze strayed to a wall where a large-framed watercolor hung beneath a skylight, but she couldn't focus on anything beyond the brightly hued drawings in front of her.

"These were done by some young friends of mine," Trent explained softly. "Kids I spend a lot of time with."

"I see," she said, but she didn't. Now that she thought about it, he didn't look like the paternal sort at all. So why did he display the amateurish art of a group of kids he spent time with?

"This way," he said, interrupting her careening thoughts, again reminding Miranda why she had come. They wound their way around several piles of heavy rope, boots, crampons, carabiners, and an ice ax. She recognized the equipment because she'd once considered taking a mountaineering course.

"Hiya, Toots!"

She jumped, then spotting the croak's source, walked over to a curtainless window. From its ornate, floor-to-ceiling wicker cage, a bird glared at her with black-eyed absorption. "Hiya, Toots," it repeated, sounding irritated.

She decided to humor it. "Hello there. How are you this beautiful morning?"

"Damned knee hurts like hell," the bird cursed, limping along the wooden bar.

Miranda covered her mouth after a short burst of laughter. It was obvious where the bird had learned that.

"Behave yourself, Karnac," Trent ordered, coming up behind Miranda. He poked one finger through the bars to stroke the mynah's black head and rusty wine-colored back.

"I bite."

Trent joined in Miranda's laughter, but withdrew his finger. "Tell me about it, you ornery cuss. Now, introduce the lady to your pal."

Only when he reached around her to scratch its chin did Miranda notice the cat. Draped over the top of a carpeted, multileveled perch, a sleek Siamese ignored the commotion.

"Liver lips," Karnac taunted, but the cat merely closed its eyes, which were sleepy and blue-gray like its owner's.

"I didn't think a cat and bird would tolerate each other," Miranda marveled, shaking her head.

Trent guided her away from the bizarre menagerie. "Surprised me, too, but I guess when Cromwell decided to adopt us, he figured this was a package deal and he had to put up with all of us. Me, the bird, and the fish."

"There must be stories behind those names."

"Karnac belonged to my sister. She's convinced he can read minds. Now that I've had him for more than a year, I think she might be right. As for him," Trent went on, aiming a thumb at the cat, "he demanded entrance one freezing night last January. He looked like he'd never lost a battle so it had to be Cromwell."

They walked by a modern glass and lacquer dining table large enough to comfortably seat ten. The companion chairs, silk-cushioned Chippendale and genuine antiques, were several yards away, arranged in a haphazard semicircle facing a wall of aquariums. Through bubbling water and colorful darting tropical fish and other sea creatures, Miranda got a distorted view of the kitchen.

Trent skirted the long breakfast bar littered with blackened banana peels, an overturned milk carton, a dusting of crumbs and, particularly revolting, a crusted can of chili. "Oh, yuck." Miranda gave the bar's repulsive bounty a wide berth.

"Midnight snack," was how he described the carnage.

"Must have caused you terrible nightmares," she said dryly, giving the can of chili one last scornful glance.

"Spare me from food snobs," Trent grumbled, but she heard a smile underlying the disdain.

When he turned to rummage through disorganized cupboards, Miranda gaped. A long scar bisected his otherwise smooth back, and she gritted her teeth at the pain he must have suffered. What had happened to produce the angry, roseate slash that paralleled his spine? The same thing that damaged his knee? It was disconcerting to realize that she felt both curiosity and compassion for him.

Miranda concentrated on his search, wrinkling her nose at the stacked array of beef stew, SpaghettiOs, Vienna sausages, chow mein, and soup. He finally located what he was looking for and handed her a small jar. She stifled the impulse to shudder. Trent needn't worry that anyone would accuse him of food snobbery. Miranda held the instant coffee with two fingers, gingerly, as if he'd passed her a grenade. There was no diplomatic way to tell him she'd sooner down hemlock than this instant coffee.

The stuff had solidified and turned almost black. Did he really think he was doing her a favor? She raised both brows.

"Sorry. I don't drink it." He lifted his shoulders and smiled disarmingly. "Guess it's been around awhile."

"About a decade, from the looks of it."

"Someone truly desperate for caffeine could add hot water and salvage enough for this morning."

"Trust me. No one could be that desperate." She handed the jar back to him, deciding to forego a short lecture on the benefits of freshly ground coffee. People who didn't have the proper respect for it were never convinced. "Thanks anyway. I appreciate the thought, but I'll take a rain check."

Fearing that he might assume she wanted to see him again, Miranda bustled toward the door.

"I'll hold you to the rain check, Mandy. And soon."

In her haste she almost collided with a weird-looking chair. Because she'd tried one out in a posh San Francisco shop, she knew its name sounded like some dinosaur, and that the down-filled leather cushion felt divine when it conformed to aching backs. It also cost nearly as much as a small sedan. In direct contradiction to the chair's opulence, a tiny-screened black-and-white television rested on a cracked plastic tray, blaring out the daily dose of disastrous news.

But the man who lived here was the biggest paradox of all. Spacious as the apartment's interior was, Miranda felt pressured to get away. Trent's presence crowded her, confused her, kindled a fight-or-flight reaction, even though he hadn't said or done anything threatening.

"Run for your life, honey. Trent's a stud."

Trent's explosive laughter punctuated the bird's absurd warning. Miranda scurried even faster for the door, and safety. A hand on her shoulder thwarted her escape.

"Don't pay any attention to Karnac. That speech is my sister's idea of a joke."

A joke? Sure. She didn't believe for a minute that his sister just made that up. "You probably are."

"Probably am what?"

"A stud." Miranda touched her flaming cheeks and prayed that he'd gone temporarily deaf. Of course, such selfish prayers were doomed to go unanswered.

Trent squeezed her shoulder once, twice. "Well, now, I guess you'll have to find that out for yourself, Mandy."

So much for sweeping exit lines, Miranda berated herself seconds later as she jabbed the elevator call button. All she'd been able to mumble was "I told you, it's Miranda." What was it about Trent that made her say and do such disturbing and unpredictable things?

Bypassing her floor, Miranda went to the lobby, straight to a row of brass-faced mailboxes. There were four plaques for every floor, each with a last name, two initials, and an apartment number. For the fifth floor, there was a single box and it read only FARRADAY. No initials, no number, just one name.

It was disquieting to think of Trent living right above her, so close, she might hear his footsteps, hear water running when he showered. And if her bedroom was under his, she could hear him . . . No, mustn't think about him and the women he entertained.

Who was Farraday, and more importantly, what was the relationship to Trent? She was positive she didn't know anyone by that name, except a niggling sense of recognition flitted somewhere deep within her memory. After checking her watch, she uttered an impatient groan and dashed down the stairs to the underground garage for her car. Talk about late! She didn't have time for useless speculation about either Trent or some absentee owner.

But all during the drive down Broadway, she couldn't get it off her mind. Why did Farraday sound so familiar?

"Miranda, you could pack enough in those bags under your eyes for a round-the-world cruise," Sam Callahan said in his customary blunt manner. "Do you ever sleep?"

Not enough, she admitted silently, and hardly at all last night after her first encounter with Trent. Because of all her boss had done for her, Miranda put up with his benevolent meddling. "It's so nice to have you back, Sam. No one else can give me an ego boost quite like you."

"Hah!" he barked, sweeping aside a stack of papers that had accumulated during his two-week absence. "Your ego isn't on the agenda. And don't think you can get around me by changing the subject. I know you too well."

"I can't dispute that." Miranda watched in fascination as Sam burrowed under piles of folders to extricate a scarred brier pipe. She was continually astonished that a man with such an incisive, analytical mind could function amidst this self-generated chaos. After locating his tobacco and a box of kitchen matches, Sam once again concentrated on her.

"Now, I've called you in to talk about when you're going to take a vacation." He struck a match with flourish and fixed his gaze on Miranda's stunned face.

"Sam, I spent the whole first week you were gone trying to convince Forester-Cavanaugh that they can't do without our services. And you want to discuss my going away?"

"Ouch!" Sam dropped the match, which had burned down and singed his fingers. "Lucy will have my hide for this," he lamented, probing a small hole in his jacket.

Miranda smiled at Sam's reference to his wife. Lucy Callahan selected her husband's wardrobe with taste and dedication. In spite of her efforts, he regularly ventilated the fine fabrics with fallout from his pipe or matches. Sam had the habit of striking a match, then continuing to talk until it burned him and he flung it down in a hail of curses. The routine was familiar to anyone who'd known him longer than five minutes.

"Can we get back to business? Aren't you interested in whether I was successful in selling Forester-Cavanaugh our consulting package?"

Sam's smile around his pipe stem was ironic. "I never worry about your being successful, Miranda. When you decide a company's executives or sales force need your motivation seminars, it's only a question of when they agree, not if."

After several aborted attempts, he succeeded in lighting the pipe, and puffed reflectively for a moment. "Look at how you coerced me into creating a whole new department of Callahan Associates, tailor-made for your talents."

She absorbed the small jolt his words dealt her. "I never dreamed that you saw it as coercion," she said very softly. "I hope you don't think I'd ever do anything damaging to this company. You, of all people, know how much it means to me."

Sam had given her the opportunity to make her dreams reality. He'd gone to her high school to give a motivational speech, and a few weeks later, she'd bravely marched into his office and pleaded for a job. In return, she promised to work for him for the rest of her life. Though Miranda didn't like owing anyone, her debt to him was incalculable. She'd never be able to do enough to fully repay his generosity and confidence in her.

Sam squirmed at the distress in her voice. "Thunderation, Miranda!" He tossed the pipe into an ashtray, slapping at a few errant sparks that showered onto his blotter. "You're probably going to take this wrong, but that's the trouble. Callahan Associates means entirely too much to you. When did you—"

"Please," she interrupted, raising one hand in protest. "Not another speech on the evils of 'all work.' It isn't a valid argument anyway. I eventually use all my vacation."

"Sure," he conceded with a mocking twist of his mouth. "But do you go somewhere and take it easy? Do something different? No! You chase off on some study tour that you've done weeks of homework to prepare for. You sit in classes or march around to sights like a recruit in basic training. What kind of vacation is that?"

Sam wasn't the only person who disapproved of the way she spent her time off. Friends were forever telling her to forget self-improvement and go for thrills. "There's nothing wrong with educational vacations," Miranda said in defense of her choices. "I've learned a lot."

"No doubt. But haven't you ever thought about

holing up on some nice tropical island where the most strenuous activity would be bending your elbow to lift a drink?"

"Why, no," she confessed honestly. "I wouldn't—"

"Learn anything? Maybe not." He reclaimed the pipe. "On the other hand, you might learn how to relax. Whether you realize it or not, Miranda, you need that more than most. Hell, I'm no shrink, but I can see you've been pushing too hard, too long. It'll catch up with you."

He leaned across his desk and gave her hand a paternal pat. "Take some advice from an old war-horse. Balance that restless drive of yours. Find something, or better yet, some*one*, to give you pleasure."

Miranda hurried back to her office and sank into her chair. She closed her eyes and massaged both temples to soothe an incipient ache that threatened to develop into a full-blown throb. Sam's parting words hammered at her. *Learn how to relax. Balance that restless drive of yours.*

His final admonition, however, had her stomach doing crazy flip-flops. When he told her to find some*one* to give her pleasure, she'd had a fleeting but vivid image of Trent in some woodsy retreat, beckoning to her. Now, there was a man who'd never have to be told to take it easy.

She jumped up to pace between her desk and the window. This constant dwelling on Trent—she didn't even know his last name—had to stop. It interfered with her sleep and was now hampering her ability to work. Just when she had urgent issues to deal with.

Why couldn't Sam and Leslie and everyone else

accept that she was content with her life the way it was? Someone was always advising her to "do this, don't do that," when in fact she was doing exactly what she'd always wanted.

Granted, everything she accomplished, each goal attained, only made her add more goals to her list. But how else could a person grow and succeed? One had to continually set new goals and be unwavering in the pursuit of them. Miranda had learned that lesson early in life, and would never allow herself to forget it. She was terrified of ending up back where she had started. She'd climbed too far to fall.

Perhaps to someone who hadn't overcome so many obstacles or struggled so long, the job and its title or the apartment and its prestigious location would mean little. To Miranda they were rewards, vindication that her work and sacrifice had paid off.

She let out a weary sigh. Maybe Sam was right, and a vacation was the ticket. She had been tired of late, and more often than not she relied on makeup to conceal the shadows caused by insomnia.

Remembering the foreign study tour to the Galápagos and Easter islands, she consulted her calendar, and frowned. It was well past the deadline for reserving space. How had so much time gotten away from her? She hated neglecting even the smallest detail, and here was a major slipup glaring her in the face.

Luckily no similar error had ever occurred in her work. She was proud of her reputation; her record was enviable. Miranda glanced at the IN basket, full to overflowing as it invariably was after a week out of town. There was no vacation in sight for her yet.

"You're always in such a hurry, Mandy. This may sound trite, but don't you ever stop to smell the roses?"

Late for a Saturday morning exercise class at her health club, Miranda had rushed off the elevator and straight into Trent's arms. She told herself she ought to step free of those arms that were still loosely wrapped around her. And she would. Soon. She told herself she didn't like the rugged outdoorsy lure of him. But she did. Undeniably.

He looked even better than she remembered because she hadn't seen him in nearly two weeks. She'd studiously avoided him, leaving for work very early in the morning and staying out late at night. Though she refused to admit it, she was disappointed at how easily she'd accomplished her goal, almost as if he, too, were trying not to run into her.

Though she knew she shouldn't be encouraging him now, Miranda couldn't help smiling at the message on his T-shirt. IT'S NEVER TOO LATE TO HAVE A HAPPY CHILDHOOD. When he snapped the elastic of his red suspenders, and with a wink said, "No danger of losing my jeans now," she laughed aloud. It felt good.

Her sister wouldn't mince words. She'd come right out and say Trent was a fine piece of body work. No, medical school had made Leslie crude. Her description would likely be more anatomically correct. But men, especially men like Trent, didn't inspire such reactions in Miranda. Yet here she stood, vibrating with a need to trace the dimple in his left cheek, to test the texture of his beard and see if it felt scratchy against her face.

Instead of indulging her whimsical wish, she looked all around the tastefully furnished lobby. "Lead me to the roses and I'll be glad to smell them. On my way out."

"Tell me," he demanded, his expression sobering, "does this lady-of-the-manor routine usually do the trick?"

Her back stiffened. "I don't know what you mean." But she did know. She understood perfectly that she resorted to flippancy as a defense when someone got too close. Miranda suspected he knew it too. She took the delayed steps away from him, and Trent's hands trailed down her arms. Visually caressing, his eyes wandered from the scooped neckline of her hot pink leotard, over the teal wraparound skirt, back up. When he rubbed the heel of his hand over his stubbled jaw, goose bumps dappled her arms.

"I mean, are most men intimidated by your wicked tongue? Do they skulk off to a suitable distance after you zing them with those sweet little put-downs?"

"They do if they're gentlemen," she snapped, treating him to a full measure of the condescension he'd accused her of. "A concept probably unfamiliar to you." More than once since meeting Trent, Miranda had caught herself sounding haughty. There was just something about him that rubbed her the wrong way and made her say the wrong things.

His laugh surprised her. "You're right about that. Even the word 'gentleman' sounds a whole lot tamer than I ever plan to be."

Miranda didn't need any reminders that tame

and Trent were contradictions in terms. His physical presence was proof enough. Too easily, he goaded her into being prissy and critical, and he relished doing it. She seemed to amuse him, and that was something Miranda couldn't tolerate.

"You're rather presumptuous for a—"

"Lowly handyman?" he finished, unoffended.

She stared at the leaded glass door, marshaling her thoughts. She had intended to warn him that she'd speak to management if he didn't stop bothering her. But she knew he would find that an empty threat.

She tried a different approach. "Trent, I admit that I sometimes act, uh, high-handed. But I can't figure out why you keep trying to shock me and make me ill at ease."

"Can't you, Mandy? Can't you tell when somebody wants you to take notice? To look at him as a man. He'll stoop to just about any tactic that will work." His thumb outlined her lower lip. "I'm no different. If I acted polite and deferential, as you apparently think the hired help should, would you give me anything except an equally polite response?"

"I—"

"We both know you wouldn't." He tipped her chin up. "So, like an adolescent, I resort to teasing and showing off to get a girl's attention, then disappearing to make your heart grow fonder." His eyes appeared quite blue and intent. "I'm chasing you, Mandy."

The confession left Miranda speechless. It also stirred up a whirlwind in her stomach strong enough that she longed to escape.

"Now, if you were to loosen up a little," he continued, "give me the attention I deserve, I could stop acting outrageous." He shot her what she assumed was supposed to be a contrite look. But no way did it override the grin hovering around his lips or the devilment in his eyes.

Miranda chuckled, aware of how easy it would be to fall victim to his masculine appeal. "I bet you think all you have to do is flash that dimple and you can charm my socks off."

"I'd rather charm your pants off."

"This from the man who only seconds ago promised to stop acting outrageous?" Pleased that she wasn't blushing, Miranda shook a reproving finger at him. "You have a pretty wicked tongue yourself, Trent."

He showed her just a flash of it. "You don't know the half of it, Mandy."

Three

"You're going where?" Leslie Hart gasped, flushed and panting from the exertion of doing one hundred leg curls on a sadistic chrome monster.

Miranda eyed her sister from an identical machine that was punishing her even more because of additional weights. "You don't have to look at me as if I just announced I'm off to live among the natives of Borneo. I merely mentioned that I'm going on a picnic in Swope Park."

Leslie sat up and mopped her dripping face with the sleeve of her plain old-fashioned black leotard. "Mandy, the probability of you going to Borneo is significantly greater than the likelihood of your roasting wieners in Swope Park." She scrutinized Miranda for a few seconds, then shook her head. "You'd better come in for a checkup. There must be something wrong with you."

Miranda wished she could dispute that, but Leslie's diagnosis was on target. Something *was* wrong with her, rendering her unable to think or act logically. Otherwise, she'd never have let Trent coax her into an outing with him. Especially after he had told her the picnic would include a group of inner-city kids. He must have offered that information as an incentive, probably thinking she would view the young chaperons as protection. He couldn't know that confronting her with reminders of her own childhood would be more disturbing than reassuring.

And yet, she'd consented to meet them at one o'clock. Consented after only a token protest. Consented and volunteered to bring all the makings for homemade ice cream, including a freezer that she would have to buy.

"Premature middle-aged crazies," Miranda mused, rising with the gracefulness that was the by-product of a well-conditioned body. "Too bad there's no medicine for it."

Leslie groaned and struggled to her feet, trailing her sister to another instrument of torture. "What prompted this urge to commune with nature?"

"Les, if I had an answer for that, I'd tell you. But this guy just hangs on like a bad case of static cling."

"Oh, a guy. Let me guess. Can it be . . . Filbert, your opera-loving stockbroker?"

"Fielding. Symphony. Lawyer," Miranda corrected, resigned to playing one of Leslie's games. "And, no, he's in Europe for an international legal symposium." She adjusted the tension on the apparatus and began a paced set of pumps.

"Bad guess anyway. Filbert couldn't go on a picnic. He wouldn't be caught dead wearing anything other than pin-striped suits." Les sent her sister a look of bland innocence, then ruined the effect by adding, "Except maybe pin-striped pajamas."

"I wouldn't know about the latter," Miranda said, coolly quashing Leslie's subtler than usual probing into her love life. "We go to the Philharmonic, not to bed."

Les guffawed. "Of course. Wonder why I forgot that?" Her index finger shot up. "Then it must be the fast-food mogul who feeds you hot investment tips. What's his name? Kermit?"

Miranda sighed and bit back a smile. The things one had to put up with from a kid sister. "Kirby. Who, as you know, owns a chain of health food stores, and shares his Royals and Chiefs season tickets." She gestured for Leslie to get busy doing arm extensions. "Who, as you also know, told us a week ago he was heading to the Canadian Rockies for the last skiing of the season."

"Ah, yes. Now I remember Kermit's ongoing flirtation with compound fractures." Les scratched her head, a transparent ploy to delay further exercises. "So who's left? Surely you're not dining alfresco with fussy old Waldo. I hate to tell you this, Mandy, but I'm afraid ants will terrorize that man."

"Walker isn't fussy. He's refined. Just what you'd expect from a museum curator who has forgotten more about art than I'll ever learn."

Leslie's loud snort was followed by a leer. "Yeah, but does he induce heart fibrillation and sweaty palms?"

Hardly. Only one man could accomplish that, Miranda thought, then said wryly, "Delightful as it sounds, my relationship with Walker is confined to our mutual interest in art."

"Tell me something new. When has your relationship with any man ever gotten past your shared interests?" There was a clank as Leslie thrust her arms outward and sent the weights crashing. "Unless they can teach you something you want to learn, you don't waste much time on the male of our species. You ought to forget picking their brains, kiddo. Try jumping their bones instead."

Miranda ignored the tasteless advice, opting for a lecture on the importance of keeping each facet of life in its proper place. Leslie planted both hands on her hips, silencing her sister with a ferocious scowl.

"Honestly, Mandy. Haven't you ever met a guy and been hot to ravish his body, to hell with his position, his degrees, or his interests?"

"Certainly not," Miranda denied vehemently, uncomfortable with both the lie and the awareness of how many times she'd fantasized about doing exactly that with Trent. He had a look about him that spoke volumes. And it fairly screamed that the things she could learn from him had no place on her self-improvement list.

Knowing if she didn't change the subject Les would keep at it until she'd ferreted out every detail, Miranda grabbed her sister's wrist to tug her toward the dressing room. "Let's hit the whirlpool."

"I know just the guy you ought to meet," Leslie went on, unfazed by the minor diversionary tactic. She elbowed Miranda in the ribs and winked lewdly. "Trust me, Mandy girl, this one could really heat your sheets."

"I hope you don't say things like that to your patients," Miranda scolded, covering her ears against a sudden piercing noise.

Her unmistakable relief didn't escape Leslie who grinned and depressed a button on the small black device clipped to her belt. "Saved by the beeper, sister dear. But don't think I'll forget where we were in this discussion. I will get you fixed up, and you'll be glad."

Several hours later Miranda eased her Volvo into a gap in the park's congested traffic flow. She'd probably never find Trent and his group even though he'd given her instructions about where to meet them. No doubt he treated directions with the same nonchalance he accorded everything.

She rolled the front windows down, taking in the scene on both sides of the road. The first really warm day had winter-weary Missourians streaming in droves to the large city park, intent on making up for months of indoor confinement. Miranda saw every imaginable kind of game being played with manic energy. There would be plenty of sunburns and sore muscles tonight.

She thought back to her initial meeting with Trent. His languid way of moving and talking had misled her into believing he was lazy. Then she'd seen him in that poor excuse for shorts and recognized the sleek lines and well-developed muscles of an athlete who worked out consistently. His body wasn't that of a man who spent his time on household maintenance.

Miranda replayed her sister's parting words. Just this one time maybe she should give in to Leslie's matchmaking attempts. She wasn't looking for even the most casual kind of relationship, but it might serve to get her mind off Trent. These days almost everything reminded her of him. She needed a distraction, a powerful one. A sheet heater maybe? She pushed in a cassette, and her laughter mingled with the soft sounds of a Debussy prelude. What else could she do but laugh at such a ludicrous idea?

Lately, Les had gotten fanatical about finding Miranda the right man, as if she were now the adviser and protector. But after so many years of working to ensure her baby sister's success and happiness, Miranda found it difficult to relinquish that role. She'd always looked forward to the time when Leslie would be completely independent. That time had come, but where was the elation? Perhaps she needed practice at being self-absorbed.

Trent could give her lessons. He epitomized the carefree lifestyle. Everything about him, from his singular way of dressing to his attitude toward work, was blasé. He mooched free rent, dropped out of sight for days, and didn't appear to be pursuing any long-range goals. Miranda couldn't identify with or condone such lack of direction.

"Why are you doing this?" she chastised herself, slamming on the brakes to avoid rear-ending a station wagon overflowing with Girl Scouts. "It's his life." Aside from this excursion it had nothing to do with hers.

Immersed in her pep talk, Miranda almost drove past him. Unbelievably, he motioned her into an empty parking place next to where he stood. Because there was a steady parade of cars seeking slots, she wondered what form of intimidation he'd practiced to save the spot for her. Probably the same kind of voodoo spell he'd cast to get her here in the first place. She unbuckled her seat belt, got out of the car, and walked toward Trent. He was leaning against a black Suburban with his elbows braced on the hood, and one foot propped on the bumper.

"You look good," he said in greeting.

"Oh . . . thanks," Miranda replied, dismayed. She purposefully had not styled her hair after taking a shower, letting it dry naturally into fine wisps that framed her face and neck. Then she'd chosen a simple, pale gray jumpsuit and applied a minimum of makeup. She would never go out looking like a witch, but today she hadn't taken the usual pains with her appearance. Apparently the ruse had backfired. Trent thought she looked good, and had told her so in his usual disconcerting way.

"You're welcome." He smiled, as if he saw right through her attempt to make herself unattractive to him. "I like the outfit, and your hair done that way. You look much more accessible."

Just what I need. To be more accessible to Trent.

"Relax, Mandy," he urged softly, fondling the button on her epaulet. "I'm chasing, but when I catch you, it'll be because you've slowed down to let me."

"I hope you handle disappointment well," she told him, careful not to let the internal tremors she was feeling creep into her voice. "That's never going to happen."

"You underestimate me. But that'll work in my favor too." Cutting off Miranda's indignant protest, Trent steered her back to the Volvo. "Unlock the trunk and we'll haul some of the stuff over to our tables. After you meet the kids, I'll have some of them come back for the rest."

Together they lifted the large cooler and carried it to the picnic spot. With each step, Miranda told herself it was the thirty pounds of crushed ice that weighed her down. But it was dread. Stomach-churning, mind-numbing dread.

In the course of her work, she often stood alone on a stage and promoted self-motivation to hundreds of people. Not once had she experienced the kind of terror that gripped her now. If she didn't get control of herself, she would be in the throes of an anxiety attack. All because of a group of children who'd escaped the inner city for a few hours.

Miranda breathed deeply and concentrated on slowing her hammering heart. At last her determination took over and she was able to hold the panic at bay. She knew that her smile might be a bit tenuous, but it was better than scampering off like a spooked animal. She accepted Trent's outstretched hand, and he led her toward a noisy soccer game.

He had to blow the whistle twice before play was halted. Eight pairs of interested eyes focused on Miranda, and the curious youngsters gathered in a semicircle around the two adults.

"Okay everybody, I want you to meet Miss Hart," Trent said, leaving her side to touch each child as he told Miranda their names. They were a racial mix of boys and girls, ranging in age from six to ten. Several, overcome by shyness, bobbed their heads and averted their eyes. Others mumbled what passed for a greeting. But one little girl, much tinier than the rest, marched up to Miranda and offered her hand.

"I'm pleased to meet you, Miss Hart. You'll have to excuse them," she said, flicking a critical glance at the rest of the group. "They sometimes forget their manners."

Trent had called her Bird, and the name was appropriate. She looked small and fragile, as though a strong gust might carry her away. But the minute she'd come out with that very proper, very grown-up response to the introduction, Miranda knew that Bird took herself very seriously indeed. And expected the same of everyone else.

The dignified little sprite struck a poignant chord in Miranda, relieving some of her earlier misgivings. She sensed that the two of them shared more than a few traits in common, and found herself hoping Bird would find a role model who'd inspire her to get the education that could guarantee her a better life, as Sam had done for Miranda. "The pleasure is mine, Bird," she said, smiling as she returned the firm handshake. "I appreciate all of you letting me join you today."

Trent ruffled two of the boys' hair. "What do you say, gang? Miss Hart tells me she hasn't been on a picnic in a long time. Shall we show her how it's done?"

An enthusiastic chorus of, "Yeahs, you bets, and all rights," hailed his suggestion, and the youths swarmed around the table like bees drawn to clover.

As they set out the food, Miranda had to revise her opinion about Trent's eating habits. The frankfurters were from a kosher deli, the buns five grain, and there was a large selection of vegetable and fruit salads, accompanied by gallons of lemonade.

When she commended him on his selections, he informed her that just because he chose to eat out of cans didn't mean these kids shouldn't learn something about good nutrition. Miranda nodded, surprised to find a subject on which they agreed.

Lunch conversation revolved around school, with Trent questioning each child about his or her activities. Miranda was on the verge of swallowing her last bite of hot dog when one of the boys astounded her by insisting that Trent tell them about the mountain he'd recently climbed.

Mute, she stared at him, absorbing the reason he'd been gone all last week. Mountain climbing. One more revelation, one more indication that her first impression of Trent might have to be revised.

She listened as he downplayed the danger, stressed the necessity of having the best equipment, of being prepared and above all, cautious. "Accidents happen to those who take foolish chances." Then as if he didn't want to be the center of attention any longer, he demonstrated how to pack the freezer with ice and rock salt, and said to Bird, "Get cranking."

The homemade chocolate ice cream was a big hit, especially since everyone had a turn at the crank. Jay, a little boy who'd been too bashful to talk to Miranda earlier, asked if they could do it again soon. Without a second thought she assured him they could. Belatedly she realized she'd committed to more than another session of ice-cream making. She'd agreed to see Trent again.

When most of the food had been devoured, Miranda and the girls challenged Trent and the boys to another round of soccer. After an hour of cutthroat competition the score was tied, so Trent called the game and sent the kids off to the playground.

"Whew," he panted, collapsing onto a bench. "My thirty-four-year-old bones can't go the distance with those younger ones."

"I know what you mean," Miranda said, blotting

her face with a paper napkin. "And I thought I was in pretty good shape."

"You are in good shape. I felt it when we collided out there. You're supple and strong. But, ah, Mandy, where it counts, you're soft. I felt that too."

The illusion of safety dissolved in an instant. No longer could Miranda rely on the children as buffers against Trent's potent sensuality. She'd allowed an innocuous outing in the park to lull her into a false sense of security. How could she have forgotten the hazards of being anywhere near this man?

She latched on to the first thing she could think of to divert him. "Do you do this often?" Miranda's gesture took in the picnic table and energetic youngsters.

"Every chance I get," he said, allowing her to change the subject. Trent fixed his gaze on the hazy sun beginning to disappear behind the tree-tops. "It's mandatory for me, something I'll always do. I began working with kids over a year ago. Now it seems as if I've been involved in this all my life."

"Is it a way of making up for what you missed in your own childhood?" Miranda asked the question before she considered how revealing it might be. She was acutely conscious that much of what she did now was to compensate for all she'd been denied as a little girl. There had been no trips to Swope Park or anywhere else, no time for anything but daily survival.

"My childhood? No, I don't think I missed much then. I guess my family was sort of Middle America boring. We lived in Raytown, visited my grandparents' farm, played sports, went to church camp, took family vacations. The usual stuff."

To someone who'd had it, maybe it did seem

boring. To Miranda, it sounded heavenly. And it emphasized yet another glaring difference between her and Trent.

He had no perception of what it was like with nine people living in a run-down five-room house in the wrong part of town. His parents probably hadn't ended up in early graves, worn-out from the effort of living. Nor could she see Trent assuming responsibility for a younger sibling.

"Are we talking about me, Mandy?" he asked, gently separating her from the painful memories. "Or you?"

She *never* talked about that part of her. Couldn't. She'd had years of practice deflecting inquiries into her past and could dismiss them with a minimum of words. Yet today she felt an almost compelling need to confide the whole story to a man she hardly knew.

"Trent, Trent! Jay's hurt!" The excited band propelled a wide-eyed Jay toward them.

Trent was on his feet at once, taking Jay by the hand, guiding him to the bench where he and Miranda had been sitting. "Bryan, run to the car and get my first aid kit. You know where I keep it." He spoke softly, calmly, but there was no mistaking he'd issued a command to be obeyed. Bryan sprinted off, and Trent turned his attention to Jay's injury. "Let's take a look at this, sport."

Miranda blanched at the sight of the four-inch gouge in the little boy's upper arm. It hadn't bled much, but it looked gruesome. Jay appeared to be wavering between shock and horror, and Miranda's heart went out to him.

Acting on an instinct she would have denied possessing, she sat and lifted him onto her lap, murmuring soothing words while Trent cleaned and bandaged the wound. When that was finished, they praised Jay's bravery and promised him he wasn't seriously hurt, even though the cut was probably going to hurt like the devil. Muttering angrily after learning that an exposed bolt on a slide had caused the injury, Trent set the rest of the group to packing up sacks and coolers and transporting them to the Suburban.

"How about it?" he asked Jay. "Feel like walking or do you need some help?"

"I'm all right," Jay said, scrambling up from Miranda's lap, embarrassed at being caught in what he clearly saw as a childish regression. He straightened his slender little spine and started after the others.

Frowning, Trent watched him for a time, then turned back to Miranda. "I'm going to drop everyone else off and take him to a hospital to have that checked. He probably needs a tetanus shot."

"Yes, of course. I'll take care of what's left here and call the parks department to report that slide."

"Thanks. And, Mandy? Wait for me at your apartment. We have some unfinished business."

When she opened the door to him at six o'clock that evening, Miranda had come to the conclusion that Trent was right. Things did need to be settled between them. But she didn't even have a chance to begin.

He stepped into the foyer, bumping the door closed with his heel. "Mandy."

He said only that one word, coming to her as he spoke. Miranda saw his intent, but retreat wasn't an option. Statuelike, she was incapable of moving. He bent to touch his cheek to hers, generating a riot of sensations that were out of proportion for such a simple act.

Miranda's heart surged, and her body throbbed in hidden places unaccustomed to feeling the powerful pull of a male. She wanted to resist, but try as she might, it was impossible to overrule her yearning. Trent moved, an almost undetectable shift that aligned them even closer, but kept his cheek pressed against hers.

She sighed, yielding. The beard wasn't coarse and scratchy as she'd imagined. It was amazingly soft . . . erotic, evocative. Miranda grasped Trent's arms and pressed her flushed face more insistently over the delicious abrasiveness. It didn't come close to satisfying her sudden, intense craving. She clasped her hands behind his head and treated the other side of her face to the tactile stimulation that was so uniquely masculine.

She heard Trent's breath hitch in his throat and felt the tautness of his arm muscles. His hands rested lightly on her waist, undemanding, but there was promise in the subtle pressure. Then he lowered his head.

It wasn't a kiss, Miranda told herself. It couldn't be. He merely touched his lips to hers, rubbing back and forth in an enticing prelude. No, it wasn't a kiss. There was no heat from his mouth, no dampness from his tongue. Just the same promise he had made with his smiles and teasing words.

With everything in her, she wanted what Trent could offer, wanted to seize the moment. But innate caution prevented her from giving in to the impulse. She pushed him away. "Trent, stop. I don't want this. We can't!"

He watched her moisten parched, parted lips, then lifted his eyes and looked steadily into hers.

After a long, tense interval, he nodded and walked away, leaving Miranda to wonder if the nod really meant agreement.

She followed him into the living room where he'd dropped onto the couch, looking more male than ever surrounded by pastel floral cushions. Miranda sat in one of the club chairs separated from the sofa by a low narrow table.

"Let's hear it," Trent said, as if he'd resigned himself to enduring an unpalatable sermon. "Give me all the reasons why I shouldn't be here."

Unprepared for his directness, she hesitated before saying, "I'd think the reasons would be obvious."

"To you, maybe. But I'm here. So obvious doesn't count for much, does it?"

It was hard to dispute the truth. "I admit to being curious about you," she said in her own defense. "But you must see that you're not anything like the men I know."

"That's bad?" He sounded amused, but Miranda also picked up wariness beneath the surface.

"I deal better with people when I feel comfortable around them."

He sat forward, and his gaze meshed with hers. She tried to look elsewhere and failed. "Mandy, the only reason you're uncomfortable around me is that you won't accept things as they are. You keep trying to ignore the chemistry, thinking it'll just fade away. It won't."

"But I don't understand *why* I'm attracted to you."

"Hey, I'm not such a bad guy," Trent protested. "I could probably scare up a personal reference or two if it would make you feel safer."

"I didn't mean it to sound like that." Miranda

heard her nervous laugh and searched for something to occupy her hands. "I guess I'm trying to say that you're turning out to be a lot more complex than I orginally thought."

"Actually, I'm pretty simple."

She stopped rearranging the pair of delicate crystal swans on an end table and faced Trent. "I might have believed that a few weeks ago. Today you muddied the waters."

"By taking you on a picnic with a bunch of kids?"

"No." She weighed the advantages of being completely honest and decided there wasn't much to lose. "You want the truth?" His head dipped a fraction in silent consent. "Before today I thought you looked like one of those men who model outdoor wear in catalogs. A little on the rough side, not terribly dependable on a routine basis, but useful in the kind of emergency situations you read about in fiction. You know, able to start fires, build shelters, weave ropes, recognize edible plants, and catch fish if you're accidentally stranded in the wild."

"I can do all that," Trent told her quietly.

"I'm sure you can. I just didn't view those things as being very important in real life. Now I know you can also be wonderfully sensitive with a frightened, injured child. You knew exactly what to do, and you reacted so fast. I . . . you impressed me." There was no other way to describe her reaction.

"And surprised you?"

"Yes. I hadn't considered that there might be this other side to you."

"And now that you've seen it?"

"It . . . changes things. Though I'm not sure in what way," Miranda answered, a peculiar excitement building in her. "I don't think I've ever known anyone who could qualify as a genuine adventurer."

"You still don't." He leaned across to grasp her hand. "Sometimes I like to take on new challenges. But I'm no daredevil if that's what you're implying. And I certainly don't have a death wish." He squeezed her fingers. "On the contrary. Testing myself, surviving, makes life sweeter, more valuable." Trent fell back against the cushions and stared at his hands. "It's hard to explain how badly I need that."

There was an unfamiliar element in his voice, a starkness that hinted at hard-learned lessons and things left unsaid. Depths into which Miranda didn't want to probe for fear of what she might discover. "Tell me about your latest adventure," she prompted with forced cheerfulness.

"Don't *do* that!"

"What?" The ferocity of his order startled her.

"Don't ask me those ego-stroking questions. The only thing I want to talk about is what's going on between us."

Deflated, defenseless, Miranda laced shaky fingers together and looked him squarely in the eyes. "You mean, whatever it is that makes me certain you could teach me all kinds of things I have no business knowing?" Trent blinked and sat up straighter, but his alertness didn't halt her candor. "The same thing that's making me tell you this when I ought to be keeping my mouth shut and playing the role of gracious hostess? Or better yet, showing you the door? That sort of thing?"

"Yes! Exactly that sort of thing." Quickly, agilely, he rose, stepped over the table, and pulled her up against him. "Hell, Mandy, come here. Kiss me.

You don't want to wait any more than I do." He took her lips with swift possessiveness.

Now, *this* was a kiss, Miranda thought before the last bit of her sanity fled. Nothing—not her imagination, not her dreams, not her wildest fantasies—had prepared her for the hot urgency of Trent's mouth. Nor for how willingly she matched it.

His tongue didn't seek tentative permission. It slipped boldly into the soft warmth behind her lips, circling, thrusting, suggesting. Miranda clung to him, a faint moan of acquiescence betraying how lost she was in the magic of Trent's sensual claiming.

He brought her more fully against him, and his hips began to emulate his daring tongue. His breath grated harshly in her ear. "Now tell me I don't belong here."

Miranda wrenched out of his embrace. Stricken by her recklessness, she ran her fingers through her hair, refusing to look at him. "This is insane. I'm practically climbing all over you, and I don't even know your first name."

"Sure you do. You call me by it all the time."

"Trent? But I—" She worried her lower lip, tender from his kiss. Finally she made herself ask, "And your last name?"

"Farraday."

A current of electricity rushed down her spine. "Trent Farraday. Who are you really?"

"Your neighbor?"

His questioning tone made it plain that he didn't expect her to settle for that. "What else?"

He shrugged. "How about a guy who likes to play with kids and be outdoors as much as possible?"

"All of it," Miranda demanded, crossing her arms.

"Well, darlin'," he said, holding his hands up as if being forced to confess, "I guess since I own this building, I'm your landlord."

Four

Miranda paled under the impact of Trent's announcement. She took one awkward step back, then another, flooded with conflicting emotions. First came guilt, because she'd judged him on appearance alone. Hadn't her own experience taught her how unfair that was? When she realized he'd been deceiving her, probably making sport of her, anger took hold. But equally strong—no, stronger—was resentment. Trent had revived insecurities she'd thought long forgotten.

The intervening years vanished and reflected in her ruthless interior mirror, Miranda saw a skinny, unattractive teenager. One of the outsiders. Not pretty enough to overshadow her thrift store clothes, not able to spend enough time on her studies to qualify as one of the brainy crowd, not talented enough in nonacademic areas to distinguish herself. But never naive enough to think it didn't matter. All she'd had in her favor was ambition. And tenacity.

That girl had vowed to make herself into someone who would never again be an object of scorn or ridicule. It had been years since she'd felt the humiliating sting of someone laughing behind her back. After all this time, Trent's mockery was particularly degrading.

Knowing she was overreacting, and why, didn't stop Miranda from venting her anger. "I've always had the feeling that you found me amusing," she said, her voice tight and harsh. "I had no idea just how much entertainment I was providing." She stalked over to the window, escaping him and the need to do something uncharacteristically violent. "Well, I hope you enjoyed it because the fun is over. Find someone else to laugh at."

"I would never laugh at you, Mandy."

Miranda heard the quiet sincerity in his voice and whirled around. Face-to-face she couldn't doubt the truth of his words. It was in his eyes, full of warm regard, and in his stance, open, accepting. With a flash of insight, she knew that while he might not take her as seriously as she'd like, might chide her for being too rigid, Trent wouldn't laugh at her.

Unnerved by that realization, she felt her anger fizzle like a damp firecracker. How could she rant at anyone who spoke soothing words in such a maddeningly soft voice? The thought of herself yelling like a shrew would be comical if the urge to do it hadn't been so tempting only a moment ago.

She turned away and focused on the illuminated Giralda Tower several streets away. After a long, silent interval, Miranda managed to make herself sound calm and detached.

"What reason, other than allowing me to make a fool of myself, could you have had for deceiving me about your true identity?" Under pressure, she always sounded prudish.

"It was never my intention to deceive you. At any time you could have asked and I would have gladly told you whatever you wanted to know. In fact, I'd have taken your questions as encouragement."

Miranda sensed that his rather stilted, unusually precise speech was an imitation of her own stiffness. "Then I suppose you could have interpreted my curiosity as proof your chase was succeeding."

"I'm not that much of an optimist. But I was hoping to see some sign of interest on your part."

The formality had been short-lived. She heard the familiar hint of humor in his tone and ignored it. Trent needed to understand that this was nothing to joke about. Before she could make her point, he issued his own surprising accusation.

"It was easy, wasn't it, Mandy? Easy to feel smug when you could write me off as a shiftless, part-time maintenance man. All at once that's changed. So what's going to be your line of defense in the next round?"

Had her attempts to keep him at a distance been so transparent? Miranda faced him again. He stood, relaxed but watchful, in the same spot where their torrid kiss had taken place. "Why don't we just call off the game and forget the next round?"

His eyes almost closed, and he smiled. "And have you believe I don't think you're worth the effort? Not a chance." He crossed to stand in front of her, laying one hand against her neck, feathering her cheek with his thumb. "I'm resigned to the chase taking some time. But I'm in for the duration." His thumb skimmed lightly along her lower lip, then drew down, trailing moisture along her jaw. "What are you going to do about that?"

Do? First she had to keep from pulling his thumb into her mouth. Once her urges were subdued, she might be able to come up with a reply that sounded halfway intelligent.

"Umm," she hedged, wondering how she had failed to recognize his determined streak earlier.

"My guess is that while I'm not the ne'er-do-well you first thought, neither are you ready to drag me off to that romantic canopy bed of yours."

Once again his outrageousness eased them over a tense exchange. "Not likely," she agreed, matching his smile. Yet she couldn't quite banish the image of him stretched out on her satin sheets.

"Since I'm not up to surviving a major rejection tonight, give me a big juicy kiss, then I'm gone."

Trent never did what she expected, Miranda admitted as her lashes lowered and she gave herself up to his gently insistent stroking at the corners of her mouth. Resistance melted. Her lips parted in sweet welcome.

Like a fencer's opening salute, Trent touched the tip of his tongue to hers before surging in to fill her with a sudden, fierce longing. He was all strong, compelling male, drawing forth an answering response from her most female depths. Surrounded by his warmth, the scent and feel of him, Miranda floated on a sea of sensations. Quickly, effortlessly, he lured her beyond thoughts of safety and into a realm that was dark and hot and dangerous.

Seconds later, he had pulled back and was striding away. She pressed her tingling lips together and braced herself against the window frame, shaking her head as the front door clicked shut behind him. He had wanted one big juicy kiss. He got it. More than most, Miranda could appreciate the value of going after what you wanted.

Miranda jerked off her eyeshade and tossed it onto the nightstand. The light-blocking mask hadn't helped her fall asleep any better than the warm milk she'd drunk before going to bed. Early morning light angled through the canopy, creating gauzy patterns on her coverlet. She propped herself up on one elbow, tracing the lacework reflections. Her fingers moved over the intricate design, echoing the complexity of her inner turmoil.

She was exhausted; still sleep eluded her. The encounter with the children and its accompanying memories of the past had affected her more than she wanted to admit. But it was Trent's astounding disclosure that kept her brain charging on at full throttle hours after he'd left.

He obviously thought she had discouraged his attentions because she believed him to be the hired help. Unflattering as it was, his guess had been right. Her father had been a maintenance man, a hardworking one, often putting in double shifts at the Farmland fertilizer plant, and picking up odd jobs that came his way. It hadn't been enough. In a family of seven children, there was never enough of anything.

Miranda clenched her eyes shut and covered them with her palms, as if she could block out the haunting vision. It didn't work. Years after his death, the dominant memory of her father was a pervasive grayness. Fine chemical dust had clung to his hair, his skin, his clothes, always appearing to burden him with more than its powdery weight.

In fact, it had. It had also invaded his lungs. Ultimately, it had killed him.

Her mother had died less than two years later. By then, the five older siblings had taken off, leaving Miranda with Leslie and a lifetime's worth of problems. She jerked her hands from her eyes. Why was she wallowing in the past? It had happened so long ago and was no longer important. Only the future mattered.

Trent had made it clear he intended to play a part in that future. She hadn't protested as strongly as she should have, though she knew the time wasn't right for her to get involved with any man. She had overcome the austerity of her childhood, true, but her list of goals was still too long to accommodate a romantic relationship.

So where did that leave her, aside from nursing an ill-timed, inappropriate attraction to her landlord? Miranda leaned back and tucked another pillow under her head. Though the darkness yielded no answers, her internal tug-of-war over Trent went on throughout the morning.

When the doorbell rang at eleven, she was barely mobile, still shuffling about in her robe and bare feet. Before downing three cups of coffee, she'd been in much worse shape. She hated feeling this hazy headed so late in the day. On a normal Sunday she'd be dressed and ready to go out for brunch. Trent's fault, she reasoned with grumpy malice while groping to unfasten the chain lock.

The object of her rancor stood outside the door, looking disgustingly alert and neatly dressed. Miranda raised one hand to her hair, then let it drop. It would take more than a few pats to remedy the devastation. She had stolen a glimpse of herself as she stumbled by the mirrored dining room wall.

Her hair looked like a bed of alfalfa sprouts, her face as though she had a major hangover.

Trent tapped the round lens embedded in the door. "This won't do much good if you don't peek through it before you open up. I might be a dangerous intruder out to take your . . . valuables."

He looked her over lanquidly, his eyes hot enough to scorch paper. Naked beneath the thigh-skimming silk wrapper, Miranda felt her skin prickle with unnatural heat. Her body was con-spiring against her, and desire curled into a tight-ening spiral deep inside her. "You *are* a dangerous intruder," she whispered. One who'd take more than her valuables if she weren't careful.

"Like most men, I'm only dangerous when I don't get what I want."

"What do you want?"

You beneath me. Me inside you. Right here, right now. Miranda read his thoughts as clearly as if they were her own. Then she glanced away, stunned to discover the wild, unsettling thoughts were her own.

"I'm here to take you to Sunday dinner."

"Oh," she breathed. The word sounded more disappointed than relieved. Things were really getting out of hand when she couldn't distinguish one kind of hunger from another. Miranda tugged on the sash of her robe. "I can't go anywhere. I'm not dressed."

His raised brows said, *I noticed,* but he simply turned her around and gave her a gentle push toward the bedroom. "Don't dawdle, Mandy. I'm hungry and it's already late enough that we'll probably have to wait to get a table."

Minutes later, Miranda toweled off from the

world's fastest shower. Trent was much too adroit at getting her to do his bidding, which implied that she was either too malleable to say no, or that she secretly wanted to be with him. Neither possibility was reassuring.

After partially drying her hair, she took only seconds to select a two-piece yellow cotton knit ensemble. Trent was dressed up more than she'd ever seen him, but his clothes were still casual. Even in her stupor she'd silently approved of the sharply pressed khakis, striped polo shirt, and Loafers. She stepped into low-heeled sandals while cinching a purple-and-turquoise woven belt around her waist.

Walking briskly back to the living room, she halted in front of the couch where Trent was reading the travel section of the Sunday *Star.* "How's that for record time?"

He rose and checked his watch. "Less than half an hour." As he spoke, he bent to inhale the perfume she'd dabbed at the base of her throat, tucked a strand of still-damp hair behind her ear, and brushed her lightly glossed lips with his mouth. "For this, I'd have waited a lot longer."

His every word, every gesture chipped away at her resolve. Miranda's fingers trailed down his smooth jaw. She blinked; her hand stilled. "Your beard! What happened to it?"

"I figure we're getting to the point where some serious kissing is called for. I also figure I'll need every advantage I can get." She opened her mouth. He cut her off with a cheeky grin. "Don't be so impatient. I'll see that you get all the kisses you can stand. But first we eat."

It took a lot of control to keep from laughing, something Trent made her do with regularity. She eased back, wishing she'd sent him away when she had first opened the door. Because she'd felt exposed and vulnerable, it had seemed more important that she get dressed. By doing so, she'd sacrificed her best shot at refusal. Now she had to regroup. "About eating. I'm sorry. I can't go with you."

"Uh-oh. You've been thinking too much again." He studied her for a few seconds, as if debating a course of action. "Already got a date?"

Miranda shook her head, immediately regretting her haste. She seemed hell-bent on throwing away every excuse. "But I have—"

"No other excuse. You obviously haven't eaten yet and you'll have to sooner or later." He nudged her toward the door. "Why don't you just concede these small skirmishes, Mandy, and save your energy for the really big battles."

Miranda heard herself say, "I concede. This time."

Riding down in the elevator it occurred to her that with a man like Trent, a woman could find herself giving up a never-ending series of small skirmishes only to discover she'd lost the war.

When they stepped out in the underground garage, Trent draped one arm over her shoulders and steered her to his Suburban. The vehicle wasn't old, she noticed as he opened the door for her. But its life hadn't been easy. She supposed the dents and paint scratches were a result of doing rugged duty. The day before she'd learned that his outings with the children weren't confined to the city. Several of the boys had chattered excitedly about camping trips he'd taken them on during summers and holidays.

"Where are we going?" she asked, curious when

she saw they were headed away from the Plaza area.

"Is there anyplace else for Sunday dinner but Stroud's? They're the only ones who fix chicken that tastes as good as your grandma's."

"I never knew either of my grandmothers. They both died before I was born. Both grandfathers too." The confession slipped out, as if she were accustomed to talking about her family, when just the opposite was true.

"That's too bad. You missed a lot," he said, his tone pensive. "To show you what a generous guy I am, I'll share both of mine. One is the cutest, most lovable little thing. The other barks orders like a drill sergeant. Your kind of woman."

"To show you what a generous person *I* am, I'll let that remark pass."

He laughed. "I can't believe my ears, Mandy. Are you actually teasing?"

"I like to think I have a sense of humor," she informed him with a lift of her chin. "It just doesn't show itself as readily as some people's."

He turned his attention away from driving long enough to impale her with a penetrating look. "I think a sense of humor isn't the only thing you try to hide."

"What do you mean?" She forced her gaze away from the intensity of his. The tenor of their conversations ricocheted from light to heavy so frequently that Miranda felt dizzy. And when Trent turned solemn, she turned wary.

He wheeled into the parking lot of a nondescript shingle-sided building tucked away beneath the shadow of the Troost Street overpass. After switching off the ignition, he reached over and squeezed her hand. "It means I should never initiate a serious discussion on any empty stomach. Next thing you know I'll be downright cranky. Let's go."

He was out the door in an instant, moving around to her side of the car. Miranda scrambled down and took his outstretched hand, again aware of how quickly she had grown used to Trent's touch.

His prediction had been right. They did have to wait. The erstwhile roadhouse was packed with well-dressed families who'd come straight from church, couples dressed in fashionable jogging suits, groups of senior citizens, even a few teenagers on dates. Although it was close to thirty minutes before they were seated, Trent showed no signs of the crankiness he'd warned her about. In fact, he seemed so even tempered, Miranda couldn't imagine him getting genuinely upset about anything.

In short-order time they were each served four large pieces of pan-fried chicken. Miranda ate only two of hers. She wanted to save room for seconds on the gooey, pull-apart cinnamon rolls.

"I'm glad you're a woman who's not afraid to eat," Trent said, shoving back his plate. "It's a good sign."

"Sign of what?"

"Of a healthy appetite."

She barely managed to choke down the mashed potatoes. It took all her concentration to keep a forkful of green beans from falling out of her suddenly nerveless fingers.

There was nothing inherently suggestive in his statement. And yet . . . If she didn't look at him, didn't confirm that she felt a galvanic change in the current flowing between them, she could believe Trent's reference had been about food, and had nothing to do with carnal appetites. To prove it, she reached for the last roll.

He captured her wrist and leaned over to take a bite before guiding it to her mouth. Closing her lips over the place where his had been—while he watched—was so subtly erotic, it shook her to the core. She forgot chewing, swallowing. The cinnamon flavor was lost in the remembered taste of Trent. For an insane second she wanted to throw herself across the table just so she could taste him again.

Rationality prevailed, and she dropped her gaze to his empty plate. Miranda had eaten like a growing teenage boy, but he'd easily put away twice as much. Now he was covetously eyeing her remaining drumstick and thigh. "You can't possibly hold any more." Her hand drifted down to rest on her stomach.

He followed the action, then grinned. "No, I don't need any more chicken. But Cromwell would sell his soul for your leg and thigh." He licked his lips, touched them with his fingers.

Miranda's pulse began to race, throbbing heavily against the soft cotton of her dress. Their eyes met, his dropped to measure the accelerated breathing that she knew was visible. Then he looked back into her eyes.

"Me, I've always been a breast man."

Her nervous system simply wasn't geared to withstand this game of sensual cat and mouse. She'd had enough.

"If you're going to all this trouble, Trent, just because you want a woman to sleep with, I'll tell you right now to find someone easier."

"And I'll tell you right now that if I just wanted a woman to sleep with, I'd already have found someone easier." He shook his head and rolled his eyes toward the ceiling. "I'm going to all this trouble because I hope that someday soon you'll open those nearsighted eyes and see me for what I am." He reached across the table and covered her hands, which had a hammerlock on her iced-tea glass. "In the meantime, remember your Latin. *Facta, non verba.*"

Miranda closed her apartment door behind Trent and leaned her head against the cool wood, annoyed that her hands were trembling. She shouldn't be this upset. He had merely asked her to spend the afternoon with him at the community center where he did volunteer work. For a brief time she had been on the verge of saying yes. Then she'd recalled the run-down neighborhood the center was in, and her long-ago vow to never voluntarily return to such a place.

She admired the altruism of Trent and her sister, knew that what they did was vital. How often she had wished to be brave and selfless enough to do just a fraction of the good work others did. But the prospect of going back left her feeling raw, and yes, frightened. Foolish as it sounded, she feared she'd never be able to escape again. The unrelenting hopelessness would swallow her up and all she had gained would be lost.

Unfortunately, dredging up the past was not the only thing that kept her from going with Trent. Each time she was with him, the passionate yearnings he aroused in her grew stronger, less manageable. If she didn't want to get involved—and she didn't—the only solution was to avoid him. So she had made up a little white lie and used it as her reason for not accompanying him.

"*Facta, non verba.*" She repeated the words that had dominated her thoughts during the ride home. Trent's ability to quote Latin didn't surprise her as much as it would have only yesterday. She wondered what it meant.

Miranda went to the wall of shelves in her spare bedroom, searching for a dictionary of foreign phrases. Riffling pages, she found it. "Deeds, not words; action, not talk." He'd decided he wanted her. What kind of action would he take to get her?

She spent the rest of the afternoon prowling from room to room, unable to settle down and accomplish anything productive. Ordinarily when she was agitated, her beautiful furnishings and decorative objects soothed her. Today she barely noticed all the lovely things she'd worked so hard to acquire.

It was beginning to get dark when the ornate phone jangled. She lifted the jade and brass handle. "Mandy," Leslie's breathless voice said before she could answer. "Penelope's died again, and I'm stuck at the free clinic. Can you run down and pick me up? I'm on duty at the hospital tonight."

"Isn't it time to send that Beetle to the junkyard?"

Leslie didn't bother to defend her ancient Volkswagen. "This one time only can you skip the lecture on Penelope's unreliability and get down here fast?"

"Are you all right? Miranda asked at once. The clinic was in a rough section. She worried about Leslie's safety.

"Don't fret, mother hen. I'm fine. Just need a ride."

Within minutes Miranda was on her way. How ironic that after refusing to go there with Trent, she hadn't hesitated to rush to her sister's rescue. She could justify it as family loyalty, but who was she kidding? The plain truth was Trent sent her stomach into nervous fits that had nothing to do with that other burning sensation she'd experienced lately. She supposed she ought to give in and discuss those symptoms with her sister, but she kept telling herself that mind over matter would overcome them.

Miranda parked the Volvo and locked it, glancing around uneasily as she walked toward the storefront clinic. This was no place for a woman alone, something she frequently pointed out to Leslie. Les, of course, had a sound rebuttal. Didn't Miranda often, in the wee hours of the morning, go by herself to that all-night newsstand in a sleazy part of town?

Intellectually, she knew her sister was a responsible adult, but she couldn't help feeling a mother's concern. Only natural, she reasoned, since Leslie was the closest Miranda would ever come to having a child.

Before she reached the door, Les came out toting her medical bag. Thinking her sister must be late for duty, she turned and started back to the car. Leslie caught her arm and towed her down the block in the opposite direction.

"Since you're here, there's someone you should meet."

"Leslie Gayle Hart," Miranda said accusingly, stopping in her tracks. "If this is a setup, I swear you'll be digging in that bag for painkillers."

"Don't be a dip, Mandy. Would I do that to you?"

"In a minute, you conniver. For this, I ought to

abandon you here on Tough Street." The reference was a holdover from her childhood, one she was stunned to recall.

Deaf to all threats and protests, Leslie shoved Miranda toward a dilapidated building on the corner. "Just let me introduce you. If you take an immediate, acute dislike to him, I'll give up."

She yanked open a door and pushed Miranda inside. "Shh," she whispered, holding one finger to her lips. "He's almost finished."

Shielded by a large pillar, Miranda listened to an eerily familiar message.

"Okay, everybody got their list? Who wants to be first? Tell us one thing you have going for you."

Miranda bit her lip when a faintly defiant girlish voice said, "When someone makes fun of me, I just look them in the eye and walk away. It's their loss if they can't see what a neat person I am inside." Miranda could remember a time when she'd thought the same thing. Only she hadn't had a forum like this to express those feelings.

Several others, including someone who sounded like Bird, followed with their own confidence-building testaments. The exercise was clearly designed to illustrate that no matter how much you lack, no matter what odds are against you, there is hope.

She listened transfixed as the topic switched to goal setting—how it worked and why it was important. She had no idea how long she'd been standing there awestruck when the presentation came to a rousing conclusion.

"Say it with me," the leader exhorted. "I am special. I can *do* whatever I choose, *be* anything I want." A chorus of youthful voices almost drowned out the man's softer, deeper one.

"Now before we go, take a minute and write down your goals for this week. Remember, easy doesn't count. If it's too easy, it isn't worthwhile. Anybody can take the easy route. You can be the best."

Miranda leaned against the stained wooden pillar and clasped her hands together tightly. With a few minor modifications, a few changes in terminology, it might have been her own motivation seminar. The words weren't hers, and neither was the voice. But she'd recognize that quiet drawl with her eyes closed.

It belonged to Trent Farraday.

Five

Trent watched Miranda sprint from the room as if someone had held a lighted torch to her feet. In one way or another, she'd been running from him since the night they met. He rubbed the side of his face—still beardless, Miranda had noticed. With that recollection came a smile.

While his noisy audience disbanded, Trent wove his way over to Leslie. "What was that all about?" He motioned to the now-empty doorway.

"Hanged if I know. I wanted my sister to meet you, but about the time you wound up your talk, she turned tail and ran." Leslie's crossed arms and pursed lips conveyed her disappointment. "I can't figure out what's gotten into that girl."

"I think I've gotten *to* her."

"Meaning what?"

"Meaning your sister and I have already met."

"You know Mandy? But she—" Leslie's face crinkled with glee. She fondled an imaginary crystal ball. "It's getting clearer. Swope Park. Roasting wieners. Homemade ice cream. So you're the one?"

Trent leaned a shoulder against the column Miranda had hidden behind, and smiled at Leslie's rapid-fire delivery. "Put that way, it doesn't sound like a very romantic beginning to a courtship, does it?"

"But very shrewd on your part. Mandy would bolt at the first sign of hearts and flowers. If a romantic courtship is on that cursed list of hers, it's buried at the bottom."

"What list?"

"Never mind. How did you and Mandy happen to meet? You two don't exactly hang around the same places."

"I'm her landlord." A fact that hadn't pleased her.

"The little bit of property you mentioned managing is Mandy's apartment building? You own that?"

"Don't be impressed. Your sister isn't."

"Maybe not. But she sure is in a tizzy over something. In normal social situations Mandy does not run from men. She shakes their hands and gives them a charming, remote smile that has 'hands off' written all over it."

Miranda had tried that on him too. It hadn't worked, but he liked the fact that she kept other men at the same distance. "So you staged an introduction?"

"Right. Had to get you together somehow. Mandy can be damnably elusive where my matchmaking is concerned."

"You do this often?" Trent didn't like the tense impatience in his voice. It sounded too much like the man he used to be.

"If you're asking about the competition, they're a bunch of also-rans."

"I'm not so sure about that." During the past two

weeks, Trent had watched Miranda being escorted home by several slick-looking customers. And he hadn't liked the way his gut reacted to seeing her with another man.

Leslie chuckled. "So you've seen some of her friends. Aside from being beautifully trained, they all have one thing in common. Testosterone deficiency."

Trent threw back his head and laughed. That hadn't been his problem lately. "Your sister has another think coming if she intends to treat me like the rest of her pretty boys with their fancy clothes and cars."

"I know," Leslie said with a conspiratorial wink. "But be patient. She may not see it your way for awhile."

"I'm no quitter."

"No, and neither is she. Mandy has a few blind spots, but she's also got enough courage and determination and loyalty for ten people."

"You don't have to sell me on your sister's virtues."

Leslie looked reflective for several seconds. "It comes naturally. Everything I am, from my straight teeth to the M.D. following my name, I owe to her. She gave up most of what was really important to her so I could go to medical school. That's the kind of thing you can't repay."

The quiet tribute touched Trent, but bitter experience had taught him how easy it was to lose sight of what was really important. "I want to show Mandy a different side of life, make her see it's okay to have fun. Looks to me like she needs that badly."

"I agree. So what are you waiting for? Go get her."

• • • •

Miranda cast a furtive glance over her shoulder and saw Les, trailed by Trent, coming out the door. She'd have made her getaway by now except Bird had followed her from the building. The little girl had caught up with her at the curb, and somehow Miranda couldn't bring herself to speed away and leave her standing.

"Miss Hart, I've been thinking about this since we met yesterday. I want you to give me lessons."

"Lessons," Miranda murmured, paying more attention to Trent's approach than to Bird's request. It was amazing how each time she saw the man he looked more dauntless. "What kind of lessons?"

"I want to be exactly like you," the little girl replied. "Wear pretty clothes, live in my own place, drive a nice car. So I'd like you to teach me how I can get an important job, like the one Trent says you have."

Miranda's head ached from the impact of too many shocks. What did Trent know about her job? They'd never even discussed where she worked. And how could she possibly agree to Bird's plea for guidance? She was the absolute wrong person to provide that help to a child.

Despite all the reasons against it, she heard herself asking, "How can I get in touch with you? I'll need to check my schedule and see when we can get together."

Bird's mature demeanor vanished, and she hurled her arms around Miranda's waist in an impulsive hug. "Oh, thank you. This is going to be great. Wait and see. I'll be the best pupil you can imagine."

What Miranda *couldn't* imagine was why she

had acted so rashly and how to extricate herself without crushing the girl's enthusiasm. Had she consented because she saw it as the most expedient way to escape before Trent caught up with her? Or had the force of his personality and her attraction to him influenced her to do something he'd approve of?

"Is this for girls only, or can anyone join in?" Without waiting for an invitation, Trent captured Miranda from behind. His version of a hug—arms around her shoulders, crossed lightly over her breasts, binding her to him—compounded her dilemma. This close to him, she couldn't think beyond heat and strength and possibilities. Two seconds in his presence and all her self-protective instincts flew right out the window.

Bird stepped away, beaming up at the two adults with obvious approval. Too late Miranda realized she ought not to have worried about being rude. She should have just hauled out of there, leaving behind Les and her Cupid conspiracy, Trent and his insidious charm, and Bird and her dreams. Now she was trapped by the demands of all three.

At the moment Bird appeared least threatening, so Miranda disengaged herself from Trent as unobtrusively as possible and moved toward the tiny girl. "How about I give you a ride and we'll discuss—"

"Thank you for the offer, but I'm supposed to wait here for my brother. We always walk home together." Bird eyed Leslie and Trent, then whipped out a small notebook and pen, jotted something on a sheet of paper, and handed it to Miranda. "Maybe you can call me sometime soon," she said in a hushed tone, as if she didn't want anyone to overhear.

After Miranda promised to phone during the next week, she watched Bird stride purposefully back to the tumbledown building where Trent had conducted his motivational talk. She marveled at such poise, such direction in one so young, and again, compared herself to Bird. With inspiration from people like Trent and a few breaks, there was no telling what she might achieve. And maybe, just maybe, Miranda would be able to help in some small way. She found the prospect intriguing, and wondered at her own about-face.

Fascinated, Trent tried to interpret each emotion reflected in Miranda's changing expression. Finally he gave up. It was too soon to hope she would feel the same strong commitment to helping these kids as he did.

He suspected that she, like a lot of people, believed success and happiness could be defined only in monetary terms. Hell, he'd been guilty of the same wrong-minded thinking for a long time. Learning just how wrong had cost him dearly. And two years had done nothing to diminish the cost, or the memory. He didn't want the same thing happening to Miranda.

She looked dazed, immobilized by some inner revelation. The small piece of paper she'd been clutching fluttered to the ground. "Let me," Trent said, bending to pick it up.

An agonizing pain tore up his spine, and he gasped, paralyzed by its severity. In an instant he was bathed all over in cold sweat, reeling from the dizziness that always accompanied these attacks. Damn! What rotten timing.

"Don't try to straighten yet," Leslie ordered, becoming the professional at once. Her strong but gentle hands worked on the spasm in his back, helping him to gradually stand upright again.

"Thanks." Trent sucked in choppy breaths, delaying the moment when he had to face Miranda. When he met her startled gaze, he saw the questions forming.

"I thought you said your back doesn't bother you now."

He recognized the familiar accusatory note in Leslie's voice. He'd suffered months of similar carping by assorted doctors and therapists. "It doesn't. At least, not very often." He pressed the fingers of one hand to the small of his back. "This is my own fault. I fell asleep on the floor last night. Today I'm paying."

He avoided looking at Miranda after that confession, afraid she'd guess the reason he had spent the night on the couch. He couldn't recall a time when he hadn't been able to face crawling into bed alone.

Les tapped her medical bag. "Is the pain very bad? I can give you something if you need it."

"One thing I've learned from my ordeal is that pain's relative. Once you've gotten used to living with a lot of it, these little twinges seem almost welcome by comparison. It's nothing the whirlpool and a good bed won't cure."

"A massage would probably help too," Leslie ventured, defying her sister with a sly look. "Didn't you take a course in some form of exotic massage, Mandy? Knowing you, I'll bet you're a crackerjack at it."

He saw it all in Miranda's eyes. Surprise. Indignation. And finally, blessedly, resignation. Leslie had manipulated her, but Miranda couldn't desert him when he needed help. Trent took that as a very good sign.

"I'll drive his Suburban home. You can take my car to St. Luke's." Miranda slapped a key into Les's hand. "You'll have to return it by morning because I've a ten o'clock flight to catch." Her fingers curved around Trent's arm, signaling that she was ready to go.

Trent liked the way she took charge once she made her mind up. And if he were honest, he liked knowing that being around him kept her a little off balance. Miranda prized comfort too much. Nothing wrong with comfort. It would come in time. Now he wanted her to feel the edge.

He gritted his teeth against the agony of stepping up and folding himself into the vehicle. Stretching out full-length on one of the rear seats would have served him better, but Miranda already looked apprehensive enough. No sense letting her think he was some kind of invalid, or that he was permanently disabled. Trent had other ideas about how she should be thinking of him tonight.

She drove in silence for a couple of blocks, stealing peeks at him every few seconds. He wondered if she would ever get around to asking the questions he saw hovering on her lips. "I'm not going to croak on you," he said. "It isn't so serious that I couldn't have driven myself." *But pass up a chance to be with you? Never.* "Les acts like a mother hen at times."

Miranda chuckled. "Funny, she says the same thing about me. Between the two of us, you didn't stand a chance."

"No, I guess I didn't." He wanted to keep up the banter, be cheerful and charming, but the pain was still riding him, making his voice sound strained. As he often had in the past, Trent resorted to his own form of therapy, daydreaming about something pleasant.

The rest of the way home, he tormented himself with fantasies of Miranda's hands all over him, warm, slippery, arousing. He wanted all of it, the massage and the Jacuzzi and the bed—and Miranda Hart. With each block, his body grew more insistent about the latter.

When they reached their building's underground garage, he was thankful to have his back as an excuse for walking bent over. Not until they were inside the elevator did he trust himself to stand straight.

A fresh wave of concern hit Miranda when she saw Trent's contorted face. She had tried to drive cautiously so as not to jostle him, but he was clearly still hurting. Because she had vowed to stay away from him, her first impulse had been to leave him with Leslie and her interfering ways. Yet within seconds, she'd relented. As usual. Unfortunately, giving in had nothing to do with being a mother hen. It did, however, have to do with caring, and something else infinitely more dangerous. Visions of her hands on all of him were far from soothing.

Not that she'd ever intended to carry through with Leslie's massage remedy. Miranda had enough sense not to court trouble so flagrantly. Seeing him this way, though, made her reconsider. He looked wretched.

Her hands fluttered over the elevator floor buttons. Should she make the wise choice and press four, assuring her own welfare rather than his?

Trent's blue-gray eyes met hers. His earlier pain had evolved into something different, something keener. She swallowed. So did he. "Hit five, Mandy. I need . . . the massage."

She swallowed again, but her finger obeyed the command, as if she had no choice. The realization set her already-erratic heartbeat into double time.

They entered the apartment and, as before, Miranda couldn't escape the sense of danger, the loss of control. It was nonsense, of course. She had taken charge of her life long ago and hadn't veered off target since. Trent was no sorcerer. He had no magic powers to lead her astray.

With that in mind, she could do him a favor, as one neighbor to another. Then she'd retreat to her sanctum. It was just a massage. "Where do you want it?"

"The bedroom's best."

Miranda's head jerked up. Her cheeks burned when she realized their words' double entendre. "I meant—"

"I know what you meant." He waved toward the door at the far end of the big room. "I went through months of therapy. There's a regulation massage table in there."

"Oh." She started in that direction, weaving her way around an elaborate electric train setup. A child's toy for someone who was very much a man.

Oh, she repeated silently when she stepped into the bedroom. She hadn't formed a precise picture of what she thought it would be like, but she'd vaguely expected it to exude sensuality, voluptuousness. She wasn't prepared for it to be so functional and spare.

He had a water bed, all right—his back might account for that—and it was huge. But would a man practiced in seduction sleep on white cotton sheets?

"I can't help it if this sounds like a line, but why don't I slip into something more comfortable?"

He *would* have to call attention to his jeans. They were plastered to his legs, his rear, and everything else more lovingly than anything had a right to.

"Be my guest," she said, feeling not at all benevolent. When had jeans become so mesmerizing? She didn't even like them. Give her pinstripes any day. They were safe.

Safe? Her first impression of Trent came rolling back. If this man was safe, so was a powder keg in a forest fire. She hardly had a chance to reassure herself before he returned wearing shorts. Red ones, as revealing as the blue ones had been.

Criminal! What else could she think when male legs looked that good? When seeing them made her own weak?

"How about I put on some music? It's a good relaxer."

She probably needed it more than he did. Miranda nodded, and he slid in a compact disk. Oh, no! Why did he have to pick that? His selection was the one thing guaranteed to stir her senses. Thunder crashing, rain lashing, a muted sound that might have been wind . . . or heavy breathing. She had a weakness for storms.

He handed her a bottle of oil. "Ready?"

She nodded again, and in one fluid motion he mounted the table facedown, legs spread. It was such a sexual act that Miranda clamped her legs together. Tightly. With a shiver, she let her arms hang free, shaking them to work out the tension.

When she had taken the class, she'd felt very clinical, very detached from the person she worked on. But that had always been a woman. Practicing her skills on a man was a new experience. Still, how different could it be?

Repeating to herself that muscles were muscles, she tentatively lay both hands on his back, avoiding the spine. First contact blew the theory that she could ever be clinical or detached when Trent was under her. The lightest touch sent a current of awareness racing from her fingertips to her stomach.

His skin, so smooth and tan except for the vicious scar, rippled warm and vibrant beneath her curious hands. He was hard and well-defined, with no excess anywhere. he also had the cutest set of . . .

Enough! Miranda attacked his shoulders with a vengeance. It was as far removed as she could get from that delectable backside. Pushing away the image of it bare, she kneaded strongly, working her way down but not too far down, and before long her efforts were rewarded. His breathing became deeper and more even; the tautness slowly seeped from his muscles.

She closed her eyes, letting the instinctive rhythm of her technique take over. But her mind's eye couldn't ignore his ravaged flesh. "Your back, the injury. How long ago?"

"Over two years."

He'd suffered a long time. "Wa—" A sudden, inexplicable uneasiness glued her tongue to the roof of her mouth. "Was it mountain climbing?"

Silence. Long seconds. "No. A plane crash."

"Oh, Lord." Her voice came out less than a whisper. Last night she hadn't wanted to probe. Now she couldn't stop herself. "How big? How bad?" Given his ordeal, the questions sounded inane. He seemed not to notice.

She felt his whole body go rigid. "Big enough. And ten times worse than you can ever imagine."

Just his tone painted a picture of anguish and desolation. She knew the damage had gone beyond physical. "But you survived."

"Barely, for a long time." More silence. "In the beginning, that wasn't much to be thankful for."

It was unthinkable, Trent not wanting to live. She couldn't conceive of anything so horrible it would defeat his indomitable spirit. The memories were so obviously painful that, instead of questioning him further, she concentrated on easing the tightness in his muscles.

She eased back into the rhythm. The oil warmed and slickened. The recorded storm built in intensity, erupting all around them. Heat was all around them too. He was hot enough to melt a glacier, and Miranda felt flushed on the outside, damp on the inside. She grazed a spot low on his spine, lower than she should have strayed.

Trent's moan electrified her. His hips bucked several times in quick succession and one leg drew up. Both hands crushed the towel. "Aaah, Mandy. That hurts so good."

Her skin was so sensitized that the single bead of perspiration between her breasts felt like a river. *She* felt like a river on a flowing rampage.

You can't do it. Can't! Her hands didn't obey. They framed his waist, slid up, then down, then down some more, until she was almost covering the fascinating forbidden part of him. She bent and touched her lips to the middle of his back just above the elastic waistband. When her tongue darted out, his hips pumped again. A second moist caress provoked the same reaction, only stronger, more prolonged. What would he do if she blew on the wet spot, just lightly? She experimented to see.

"No more," Trent groaned. He swung his legs around and dangled them off the table's edge. In the same motion he dragged the towel onto his lap. "Your treatment is working too damned well. I can't take any more." His breath was coming fast and rough, but no more so than hers.

Stricken by her indiscretion, Miranda took several halting steps backward. The distance separating them was charged with suppressed sexual energy. "I told myself I shouldn't come up here. That this would happen."

"This? How long is it going to take for you to admit that you want *this*?"

"But I don't," she protested, knowing the words sounded weaker than her willpower. "I have too many other things to deal with right now." She tried to conjure up her list. "I don't have time for a man in my life, any man."

He grunted his opinion of that and eased himself off the table. "Well, don't look now, darlin', but I'm already in your life. And I am hereby serving notice that I intend to stay there. For a long, long time."

Six

Miranda flew to Atlanta the morning after her narrowly averted disaster in Trent's bedroom. She carried with her a new goal, written down during the night when sleep had refused to come. Stop thinking about Trent Farraday. More to the point, stop wanting him.

She couldn't sustain her resolve for the duration of the flight. Even at thirty-five thousand feet, she couldn't escape. He dominated her thoughts so exclusively that she expected to look up and find him in the adjoining seat.

She conducted a weeklong goal-setting seminar for a large manufacturing company, but neither time nor distance could banish Trent from her consciousness.

Trying to practice what she preached, Miranda read over her own list of goals several times a day, reaffirming her dedication to her life plan. She stood in front of a mirror, telling herself the same thing she'd told Trent, that she had no room for any man. Her reflection mocked her, accused her of cowardice.

When she returned home, again she went to work extra early and stayed late, anything to minimize her chances of running into Trent. She set up an exhaustive social schedule that kept her occupied each spare moment. It served no purpose other than exhausting her.

By the following Saturday night, all Miranda wanted to do was collapse. But she didn't dare hang around the apartment. It had been almost two weeks since she'd seen Trent, which meant she was on borrowed time. For that reason, she jumped at Kirby's invitation to attend a Royals game.

Miranda had known Kirby Bartlett for several years. She also knew that she was the one woman he saw with any regularity, only because she'd told him early on that she had no interest in romance or marriage. He'd welcomed that news, and they had been friends ever since.

Tonight she tried to analyze why she'd never felt the slightest stirring of attraction for Kirby, who was unquestionably a very attractive man. He had it all. Looks, intelligence, self-made success, wealth.

It was unfortunate that her hormones had decided to act up at this late date. But if they absolutely had to, it should have been someone like Kirby who populated her X-rated fantasies.

Instead, she was hung up on Trent. What was it Les had described? Heart fibrillation and sweaty palms. Miranda had been treated to her first taste of those symptoms, courtesy of Trent. So far, she hadn't found a cure.

She was still pondering the vagaries of fate as she waved good-bye to Kirby from inside the glass door of her apartment building. Miranda could still hear the roar of his Ferrari when she spotted the elevator door standing open. She hurried to catch it, and ran smack into Trent.

His hand was on the button, as if he'd been waiting for her. "You know, Mandy, for a woman who says she has no time for a man, you sure have a bunch of them sniffing around."

That he'd been spying on her nettled Miranda almost as much as his insinuating tone. "Jealous, Trent?" She could have kicked herself for blurting out the reckless question.

"Not exactly."

She was even more incensed at how little she liked his answer. "Why not?" Damn! She'd done it again.

"Well, Mandy, this is how I see it." He hit the STOP button and halted the elevator between floors, "I'm not as jealous as I might be because I don't figure any of those guys is very important to you, or one of them would have cut out the rest. He'd be following you into bed, not leaving you at the curb."

Infuriated by his smug, if accurate assessment, she snapped, "Now, there's a classic example of male logic."

"To be expected, I guess. I am, after all, a man."

"As if I'm not all too aware of that." She almost lost it completely when he grinned.

"So, you can admit it." He crossed both arms over his chest and propped himself against the door. "Just how aware, I wonder. Shall we test it?"

Miranda stiffened, her anger instantly converted into alertness. She leaned so hard against the handrail that it cut into her back. "Test?"

"Your awareness of me."

Her whole body quaked, anticipation battling

anxiety as he closed the space between them. "Trent, this is not—"

"Does the gentleman in the thousand-dollar suits kiss you like this?"

He held the back of her head with one hand, then placed one of hers on his chest. She moistened her lips, an uncalculated invitation that he didn't need. His mouth had already descended to lay siege. His tongue forged beyond the soft barrier, an agile, clever seducer. The contact was explosive, like a sudden flash of fire.

She felt the heavy coursing inside him reach out to engulf her. His grasp tightened, exerting pressure, and he rubbed her open palm over his chest. The thin gauze of his shirt did not disguise the feel of firm muscles and silky hair. A sound, low and animallike, flowed from his mouth into hers when she brushed over small, hard nipples.

The imprint of his fingers, guiding hers, seared through the sheer cotton of her blouse, branding her breasts even though he made no move to possess them. As lost as she was in his masterful plying of her mouth, she could still hear her relentless inner voice begging for more, more.

"Does he? Does he kiss you like that?"

She had never been kissed like that. "No, but—"

"Can your dude whose car cost a hundred fifty grand touch you like this? Make you melt for him?"

She swayed as his words fell in a hot mist on her arched neck. His hand moved downward, seeking awakening each vulnerable nerve ending along her spine while his other thumb teased the undercurve of her breast. Miranda's gasp of wonder became a moan of surrender when his fingertips fanned over her nipple.

Lips, warm and pliable, caressed her forehead, her temples, her cheek, and she felt the beginnings of his beard. She touched it, welcomed it. It felt wonderful. It was Trent. Her hands speared into his hair, she nipped at his neck, sank her teeth into his earlobe. She wanted to devour him, take him inside her, keep him there forever.

"Can he, Mandy? Can he melt you?"

"No . . ." Only Trent had that power.

"The million-dollar-a-year lawyer? Does he show you he wants you this much? This much?"

Fingers splayed, his strong hands cupped the slope of her hips, then slipped lower to lift her into the cleft of his thighs. It was unnecessary to question how much *he* wanted her. The hard, thrusting evidence was shockingly real. Frighteningly real.

She struggled to pull back. "Please, Trent. Stop now. We can't. I don't want this."

He kissed her again, long and deep, as if to put paid to that claim. Then her released her. Slowly. The gradual downward slide was almost as arousing as everything else he'd done during the past few minutes.

For a while he said nothing. Somehow she'd forgotten to remove her hand from his chest. When she saw him looking at it, she snatched it away. His smile was small, knowing.

"You can stop me, Mandy. Anytime, anyplace. You can even give me a long list of reasons why we can't. But don't ever, *ever* say you don't want me. 'Cause that's a lie."

Miranda was shaking so badly, she could hear her teeth rattling. She couldn't speak. She wanted to run but couldn't do that either.

Trent's index finger rimmed her ear, drew shivery circles below it. She shook her head, more to clear it than in denial. "All my life I've made decisions based on logic. Wanting you, having you is purely emotional. It's a decision I'll never make."

His tongue made a clicking sound, scolding her. "Don't say things you'll have to take back. It's going to happen. And when it does, we're gonna love each other 'til we collapse. That's no decision, darlin'. That's a promise."

Miranda hung up her office phone, rubbing her forehead and the small frown that had formed during the conversation. Walker had just given her unwelcome news. He couldn't accompany her to the Friday night dinner honoring Sam for his contributions to the community.

She could go alone, though she preferred having an escort, and Walker was always her first choice for such functions. Dignified, reserved, and socially adept, he fit the bill perfectly. And he never made demands. Not like some men she could name.

Miranda was still fuming over Saturday night's encounter with Trent. He had kissed her and touched her intimately and inflamed her senses to the point that she wanted the impossible. In the elevator, no less. Her lack of resistance was disgraceful and dangerous. But what had kept her in a constant state of agitation was his cocky promise that they would make love.

In spite of all her protests, she was beginning to wonder if that might be the best solution. Why not admit the attraction? Go to bed with him, get it out of her system, and get back on track. Elbows on her desk, she propped her chin on both palms.

To even be considering such a course indicated how rattlebrained she'd become.

So rattlebrained that when Walker called to bow out, she had immediately thought of asking Trent to take the other man's place, an idea that was just plain dumb.

No, best to settle for Fielding, her nice, tame lawyer. He didn't haunt her night- or day-dreams.

Except that all week she neglected to call Fielding, conveniently forgetting it for reasons she didn't dwell on. When Thursday evening came, she told herself it was too late, that she preferred attending solo anyway. Then she ran into Trent in their garage and, with nary a second thought, blew all her noble intentions to bits.

The second thoughts came the minute he accepted the invitation, asking only when to pick her up the next night. Unnerved by her precipitate act, she managed to mumble a time and scurry onto the elevator. He made no attempt to follow her, but as the door closed she could tell by his crafty grin that she was in trouble in a big way.

By seven o'clock Friday night, Miranda had whipped herself into such a frenzy, she'd messed up her eye makeup three times and ruined two pairs of stockings. Her hair refused to do anything and her outfit . . .

The cream-colored silk-satin evening suit had seemed the perfect choice when she'd bought it especially for this occasion. Classy and elegant, it struck just the right note for what was essentially a business affair. Now, critiquing herself in the three-way mirror, she found flaws everywhere.

The jacket's surplice bodice dipped too low, showing cleavage. The peplum drew attention to her hips and fanny, and the skirt was shorter than she normally wore, with a back slit that exposed quite a lot of leg above the knees. The fabric rose anchored at her waistline looked coquettish.

"Oh, bother," she groused, stepping into her shoes and transferring a few necessities into an evening bag. Trent was the type who'd notice what he would, even if she were dressed in a flour sack. He'd already proven that.

Besides, with the doorbell chiming, it was too late to change.

"Oh," she said, dismayed when she opened the door and saw him. "Oh, dear." Accustomed to going out with a different breed of male, she'd taken it for granted that Trent would wear a suit. He hadn't.

His jacket was silk, very well tailored, very expensive looking. The coordinating slacks were equally impressive, as were the leather shoes. But even if he'd worn a tie, he would still be grossly underdressed. What on earth could she do about it now?

He must have sensed her distress because he said soothingly, "It'll be okay, Mandy. You'll see. I'll do most anything you ask, but I refuse to wear a tie. Nobody's got a good enough reason to make me do that."

He smiled. "I may not be dressed up, but you can take me out in polite society, and I won't embarrass you." He touched her nose, her lips, her chin with the pad of his middle finger. "Trust me."

Telling herself flexibility was a virtue, she let him take her elbow. His clothes sense might be lacking, but he had the flawless manners of a true gentleman. "History is chockfull of women who came to bad ends because some man said, 'Trust me,' and they did."

His laugh was rich, the tiniest bit naughty. "Then I'll have to take care that you don't come to a bad end."

"Hmmph!" Allowing Trent to take care of any aspect of her future was equivalent to climbing on the fast track to self-destruction. She would do well to remember that.

During their ride to the nearby hotel where the celebration was being held, he quizzed her about the time she'd spent with Bird the past Sunday.

He must have inside sources to have heard about it so soon. "I made up a list of possible activities and let her choose. She picked an Oriental art exhibit at the Nelson, then we ate at a tearoom because she wanted to go to a traditional, not trendy, place. How does someone nine years old come up with notions like that?"

"I really appreciate your taking an interest in her. That child's got what it takes to go far. She just needs some personal attention and a good role model. I couldn't have picked a better one than you."

Miranda felt a little burst of heat in the region of her heart. Sometimes he said things that simply undid her. That she had actually enjoyed the outing with Bird made his compliment all the more flattering. Even going to pick up the girl hadn't turned out to be a major trauma. "Bird is a special case. I agree that she'll probably be able to do anything she sets her mind to."

His attention strayed from the traffic for a second. "Like you?"

"If you mean each of us can design a blueprint for our life, then yes, like me." She and Bird had talked about the concept at length, and the little girl had really listened. The affinity between herself and the child had sprung up so fast that Miranda still didn't fully comprehend it.

Her acquaintance with Trent had drawn her into a number of situations she couldn't have predicted. She replayed them all while he gave the Suburban to valet parking and guided her into the lobby.

"You know where we're supposed to go from here?"

"Uh, yes," she said, coming out of her fog. "It's in the main ballroom. This way."

The crowd was large and noisy, and the mood was unmistakably upbeat. It would be easy to get lost in the crush here. But the steady warmth of Trent's hand at her waist communicated that he would not allow her to stray far.

"Your boss commands quite an audience."

"Deservedly so," Miranda replied. "Sam Callahan is quite a man. No one knows that better than I." Ignoring Trent's speculative look, she searched the sea of faces, trying to locate Sam. "There they are." She tugged Trent toward the clan, pleased that all six of the Callahan offspring had made it to the event. Not that Lucy would have tolerated anything less than a full turnout.

Sam smiled in welcome, but before she could begin introductions, he extended a hand to Trent. "Tom, good to see you out and about again. Life treating you okay now?"

"Better every day, Sam. Looks like you're not doing too badly yourself."

Flabbergasted, Miranda caught herself gaping at the two. Tom? She knew Sam hadn't made a mistake. He never forgot a face or a name. That he knew Trent or Tom or whoever the devil he was, left her speechless. So much so that she could barely stammer her own greetings.

Her brain buzzed with questions. What kind of game was he playing now? Or was it a game? Would she never draw a bead on the real man? She was certainly going to try.

As soon as they located their table and were seated, she launched her offensive. "So, are you using an alias to cover up past misdeeds?" She said it only half-jokingly.

He grinned, unperturbed. "My past might be full of misdeeds, but I own up to all of 'em. There's no mystery about the names. I'm Thomas Trent, and since my grandfather was also Tom, I went by Trent to my family and friends. When I started college, I became Tom again."

"And now you're back to Trent. Why?"

His mouth tightened, though he answered readily, in a voice as cold as ice. "Because Tom turned out to be an insensitive, money-grubbing SOB. The world is better off for losing him."

Shock waves buffeted Miranda. These bomb-shells hitting with such rapidity were making her dizzy. She had a hard time reconciling the man next to her with the one he'd described. "I can't believe you were as bad as all that."

He looked at her, dead-on. "Don't harbor any false illusions about the man I used to be, Mandy. He was every bit that bad . . . and worse."

Impossible. She'd seen him with those children, saw how much he cared, what he gave of himself.

"You've had some problems learning to like me a little the way I am now. A few years back, you wouldn't have let me anywhere near you. If you were smart, that is."

She feared the earlier disclosures were nothing

compared to what was coming. "Why do you say that?"

"Tom Farraday was hard on women."

Her stomach, which had calmed somewhat, gave a sickening lurch. Her throat felt paralyzed. "You don't mean—"

"Don't look so panicked. I'm not talking about physical abuse." He enclosed both her hands in his. "I mean that back then, I wouldn't have taken you seriously as a person, as someone who had feelings. But I'd have taken everything else you had to offer." Gently, he kneaded the numbness from her fingers. "And because I was a hotshot with plenty of bucks to spread around, I could get by with acting that way. I did it over and over."

She shook her head, disbelieving. "I just can't fathom it. A man like that is the antithesis of you in every way."

His smile was bittersweet. "That was another person in another life, but it's still part of who I am. Try to keep it all in perspective."

Throughout the evening, Miranda's mind kept coming back to what she'd found out. Functioning on automatic pilot, she swallowed the food, feigned attentiveness to the speeches, and made the appropriate responses to the glad-handing that followed. What she really wanted was to be alone, to digest this new information about Trent and how it affected their relationship. Because whether she wanted to admit it or not, they had one.

Because of that, the way Trent chose to say good night shocked her. As if he were careful not to push too hard, he left her just inside the door with the sweetest, tenderest kiss she'd ever received. Then he whispered, "Thank you for inviting me."

"You've frittered away the day mooning around here like a love-struck teenager," Miranda berated herself. "Except love has nothing to do with it," she scoffed. She adjusted the positions of two onyx panthers on a shelf. She'd puttered all Sunday, doing equally useless busywork, hovering close to the phone in case it rang. There was no reason to think it would; she didn't expect Trent to call. He never had. His style ran more to just appearing.

He hadn't done that, either, and his no-show irritated her. Even more irritating was the knowledge that if she hadn't planned the shopping trip with Bird yesterday, she'd have squandered the whole weekend. Wasting time was foreign to Miranda. Any second not spent on goal-directed action or intellectual improvement represented a missed opportunity.

But since Friday night she'd been tense and unfocused, struggling to deal with the subtle shift in her feelings for Trent. "All those times I tried to avoid you, there you were. Now I need you, and poof, you disappear." In fact, he disappeared quite often for days, never offering any explanation of his whereabouts.

She marched over and picked up her briefcase, extracting a thick folder. This was what she ought to be devoting every spare minute to. For months she'd been developing and refining the proposal. A few more weeks of work and it would be ready to benefits of leasing extra space where she could hold her seminars and have people come to her instead of her frequently traveling all over the country to go to them. If he agreed, she could earn a promotion to division head, and the kind of money-in-the-bank security she had yearned for so long.

But poring over the pages, she felt her goal fading into the background, supplanted by images of Trent. She finally gave up. "Who needs this grief?" She stalked to the closet and pulled out a lightweight jacket. Maybe some fast driving with the windows down would clear her head.

After a long session of freeway cruising, Miranda glanced at the dashboard clock, surprised to see that it was nearly midnight. She could swing through downtown, kill an hour perusing out-of-town Sunday papers, then pick up the first edition of tomorrow's *Times*. A black-and-white dose of reality would put an end to all her sappy day-dreaming.

Turning off Main, she parked around the corner from the twenty-four-hour newsstand and hiked briskly toward one of her late-night haunts.

If she entered blindfolded, she could identify the place by its smell—smoke, old sweat, and news-print. It was inhabited by a mix of derelicts, bikers, punkers, and refugees from the porno theater next door, even a few yuppie and suburban types. Those who knew her couldn't figure out why the joint appealed to her. She didn't know, either, unless she gained consolation from the unspoken camaraderie of fellow insomniacs roaming the night.

A few minutes after one, a runner popped in the

door and deposited a bound stack of morning papers. Miranda claimed the top copy, paying for it along with *Psychology Today* and a *Washington Post.* She always tried to read something from the next city on her schedule.

Facetiously wishing the sullen cashier a good day, she gathered her purchases and left. She had barely cleared the doorway when she heard voices from the shadows.

"Mmm-hmm." Lips smacked. "Lookin' good."

"Want some action, Mama? You picked the right place."

Two of them, obviously drunk. She'd been coming here for years, and despite friends' dire warnings that this would happen, she'd felt immune. Miranda quickened her steps.

"How 'bout it, sweet stuff? Tell Crash what you need."

Crash sounded incredibly young. Dare she risk a flippant comeback to imply that she wasn't intimidated? Or would they guess right away that she was bluffing?

"I don't think the babe heard you, Crash. Maybe she'd like you to come closer, whisper in her ear."

Older, colder, the second voice chilled her like a clammy hand. Shuddering, Miranda mentally transferred the self-defense course she'd been meaning to take to number one on her list. Pity she hadn't done it sooner.

Thanks to regular visits at the health club she was in good shape. But it didn't mean she could outrun them. Besides, where would she run? The only businesses open along this stretch of Main were the newsstand and porno house. Her hecklers had cut her off from both. Surreptitiously she slipped her fingers into her jacket pocket. Keys ready, she'd chance diving into her car.

"What's your hurry, baby?"

Miranda was about to hurl her papers in their faces as a diversionary tactic when a third male joined the party. "Now, boys," he said calmly, "why don't you run along. I don't think the lady's buying what you're selling."

Recognizing the voice, Miranda stopped and whirled around. Trent? Here? She must be hearing things.

"Sez who?" Crash's belligerent friend sneered, pivoting. Rough-hewn and burly, he looked the type to favor fists as his weapon of choice. She watched in horror as he forgot her and confronted Trent in a battle stance.

She started to rush forward, but before she'd taken two steps it was over. With a swift arc of his hand, Trent laid the bully flat on the sidewalk.

Crash began backpedaling. "Hey, man, take it easy. No need for violence. It was all in fun." Miranda noticed that he looked even younger than he sounded.

And Trent sounded even more unruffled than he looked. "If you're after fun, check it out someplace else."

"Uh, sure. No problem."

"Somewhere real far away, so I won't run into you again. Not around here. Not around her."

Miranda heard the aggression belying his reserve. Felt it, too, when he shoved her toward the Volvo. "Where did you learn those great moves? Can you teach me?" Now that the danger had passed, she was riding an adrenaline high. "Quick, quiet, economical, and most of all, effective. That's just what I want to learn. Can we go back to my apartment and start right now?"

He glowered at her as if she'd suggested they plot an assassination. "I think we'll go back to your place, all right. And yes, you need a lesson or two."

"I've had a self-defense or martial arts course on my list for several years. But it's hard to sign up for one when I'm out of town so much." She sounded almost bubbly. "It would be perfect if you could help me."

"We'll talk about it when we get there." He practically stuffed her in the driver's seat. "I'll be right behind you. Try to avoid trouble for the next few minutes."

Driving home was like waiting for the proverbial other shoe to fall. Once she'd calmed down a bit, it dawned on Miranda that Trent not only hadn't jumped at her suggestion about the lessons, he'd been downright surly, talking to her as if she were a wayward child.

That led her to wonder how he'd ended up there in the first place. Materializing at that particular time seemed an unlikely coincidence. Unless he'd been searching for her. If so, how had he guessed where to find her? Les, most likely. Her busybody sister had resorted to sneaky tactics before to get Trent and Miranda paired off.

Trent was hard on her bumper as she entered the underground lot and parked. Retrieving her papers, clutching them like an amulet, she walked beside him to the elevator. He jabbed four and lodged himself in the corner.

The elevator dinged as they passed the first floor. "What's with the silent treatment?"

"I'm weighing my words."

"What's to weigh?"

"Miranda," he said, very distinctly, "even a savvy, independent woman such as yourself should know there are limits. That, given this is a less than perfect world, some fates are not worth tempting."

"Sounds ominous." She singled out her door key, thinking perhaps the hands-on lesson should be postponed until Trent regained his equanimity. He was heavy into the machismo routine, and a little of that went a long way with her. "Why don't we—"

"How did you feel, knowing it was me against them? Two young hoods taking on one crippled thirtysomething guy?"

She sobered, finally understanding the message within his oblique references. It hit home more incisively than all the lectures in the world. "Horrified. Mad. Scared."

"Uh-huh. Well, let me tell you, a man whose woman is threatened feels all that and more. He wants to kill."

The icy statement was no generality. It was how *he* had reacted to Miranda in danger. Shaken, she closed her eyes. Her stomach nerves did a frenetic tap dance. The Trent she knew did not deal in violence, did not talk in terms of "his woman." But this man did. The hidden depths were turning out to be darker and deeper than she had first suspected.

Each new facet of Trent that she discovered only whetted her appetite for more. She had to find out everything about him. Knowing that the quest might put her at risk, she had no choice but to take the chance.

When they reached her door, Trent grabbed her key and inserted it in the lock, his small liberty a sign that he, too, realized they had advanced to another plane.

Feeling a little disoriented and more than a little anxious, she stepped inside and reached for the light.

Chaos and destruction greeted her.

Miranda screamed.

Seven

Objects from the hall table lay strewn about the floor. The closet door gaped open, contents dragged out and discarded. Miranda heard Trent's soft curse as he tried to keep her from charging ahead. "Don't go in there."

"I have to. Let me go." She broke free and ran to the living room. More drawers yanked out and up-ended. Couch and chair cushions flung aside. Plants overturned, leaving muddy stains on the raspberry-colored carpet.

"No!" she cried, picking up one of her crystal swans. The fragile neck had snapped when the mirrored tray had been jerked from beneath it. The mate was nowhere in sight. "Who did this to me? Why?"

Only when Trent came from the hallway was she aware that he hadn't been beside her. "I checked everywhere, even the closets. Whoever did it is long gone. Got in and out through the back door."

She expelled a quivering breath. That was why he'd tried to restrain her, in case the burglar was still inside. From what Miranda had read somewhere, she knew she was to go to a neighbor's, phone the police and wait for them to come. Instead, she had reacted without thinking, compelled by a masochistic need to see the devastation.

"My bedroom," she whispered, pleading eyes locked on Trent. Had they invaded that, too, trespassed on her most private sanctuary? His slight nod confirmed her worst fears. Again, she had to see.

Again, he tried to stop her. "Mandy, there's nothing you can do in there now. Come up to my apartment and we'll call the P.D."

She didn't listen, and he followed her down the hall. The antique lace coverlet had been ripped off her bed. One pillowcase was missing. All the drawers were turned upside down. But when Miranda spied her porcelain doll facedown in the rubble, she whimpered in anguish.

"My doll. My beautiful doll." Her eyes started to burn, and she felt a stabbing pain in her throat. Clasping it to her bosom like a baby, she rocked back and forth, refusing to look at the delicate face.

Trent's arm came around her shoulders. She felt his other hand on her cheek, heard his low, comforting voice. "She's okay, Mandy. They didn't hurt her. Look."

She risked a peek. He was right. Her most precious treasure had somehow escaped. A few tears leaked down her cheeks. She swiped them away.

One arm still around her, Trent offered his handkerchief. She pushed it back. "Thank you, but I don't need that. I am not the boo-hooing type," she snuffled. "I'm not. I never cry."

"Of course you don't."

Against her will, a steady deluge of hot tears poured from her eyes. "Dammit, never!" But she cried then. All over his handkerchief and his plaid shirt and him.

"It's not fair," she wailed, and he soothed her.

"I'll make them pay," she raged, and he agreed.

Finally, she just wept, a huge outpouring of bitter tears. And he held her, murmuring words she couldn't distinguish and promises she couldn't understand.

"Better?" Trent asked, sometime later when the torrent had finally spent itself.

Miranda gave a jerky nod, keeping her face pressed to his chest. She, who abhorred excess displays of emotion, had broken down completely. It was so mortifying, she couldn't bear to look at him.

"Hey, what's this?" He tipped her head back, forcing her to meet his eyes. They radiated such warmth and support, she nearly starting blubbering again.

"I'm sorry," she choked, sounding creaky.

"No apologies. And no self-consciousness about it either, okay? You've a right to be upset, but try to remember they're just things."

She jerked away, galled that she had sought comfort from him. "Just things to you, maybe. But if you'd ever had to do without, you wouldn't be so quick to dismiss them."

There was strength in anger, and she took refuge in it, stomping over to kick a pillow, feeling out of control for giving in to the urge. "Look around you. Even I can't tell how much has been stolen or what's merely destroyed."

Miranda bent to pick up the two halves of a

darling little bisque rabbit. Outrage ebbed, replaced by pain. She extended her palms, each cradling a piece.

"Every single thing I own is tangible proof that I bucked the odds and made something of myself. Tell me that's not important."

"I didn't mean to imply your possessions weren't important. Only that you have insurance to replace them."

"Replace? Nothing can do that." She sank onto the cushionless chair and stared into the distance, into the past. "This will sound crazy, but I can tell you exactly how long I worked to buy everything I have."

Miranda pressed the pieces together, as if she could make the rabbit whole again by force of will. "At first it was calculated—how many hours working nights at the hospital cafeteria to pay for a week's groceries. The day job took care of rent and utilities, usually. Later, I got so efficient I could count the drinks I'd have to hustle to scrape up the payment for Leslie's braces."

"Oh, Mandy. I didn't know."

She couldn't bear for him to pity her so she tried to sound glib. "The lewd remarks and wandering hands got pretty awful at times, but the tips made it bearable, and the bouncer always saw that I got home safely."

She wasn't aware he had moved until he knelt before her and wrapped her in his arms, holding on so tightly, there was no chance of escape. "I'm sorry. I had no idea. You must have felt like slugging me when I sounded so callous about the insurance. Now I'm beginning to see why all this means so much to you."

Miranda knew craving his embrace was a weakness, and didn't care. It felt too reassuring. "For years, that kind of accounting was a necessity. Now I don't have to do it, but I can't seem to stop. I fought so hard to get this far, Trent, and I can't face the possibility of ever going back. I'd die first."

He squeezed her fiercely. "That'll never happen, Mandy. I guarantee it."

"There are no guarantees. Of anything. My parents both worked so hard." She covered her eyes, trying to blot out the desolation. "It got them nowhere, except early graves. Seven children to feed and never quite enough food to go around."

Trent swore and held her even tighter, but that didn't stop the flow of tormenting memories. "We never had a moment's privacy or enough attention or fun, none of the things every child is entitled to. Without money, life is a dead end. I can't, I *won't* settle for that."

She broke the embrace and planted her fists on his chest. "If I have to work twenty-four hours a day to get what I need, I'll do it. I will! I swear I will."

Trent shook his head, his gaze searching hers. "How about love, Mandy?" he asked in a taut voice. "Was there enough of that?"

"Love is a luxury poor people don't have time for." With that assertion, righteous fervor deserted her. Struck by the enormity of what she had revealed, Miranda scooted away from Trent and crossed her arms in front of her.

He was waiting for her to say more, she could tell, but she had already divulged too much. "I can't think why I've told you all this. I've never discussed these feelings with anyone. Not another living soul."

"I think you did it because you wanted to, because you needed to. And because you know it's safe with me. I know the value of everything you give me, Mandy, and how to take care of it."

For a fleeting second when Trent's lips found hers, Miranda understood why a woman might be tempted to forsake all her goals and dreams for the security of one man's love.

Miranda watched Trent show the pair of policemen out her front door.

Because there had never been anyone else to do it for her, Miranda learned at a young age how to fight her own battles. It was a matter of personal pride that she'd done a respectable job. Her need for self-reliance was as basic as food and shelter. She equated relying on anyone else with losing control of your life, something she could never do.

But in the two hours following their discovery of the wreckage in her apartment, Miranda had looked to Trent as her anchor in the storm. He'd insisted they go to his apartment to call and wait for the officers. Once they had arrived, he answered as many questions as he could, sharing her burden. And he never left her side. She didn't know how she would have gotten through the ordeal without him.

That was an exaggeration, she told herself. She had weathered worse crises than this alone. But not in awhile. Not since she had finally begun to feel a small measure of confidence that her security wouldn't be snatched away. This incident had incited old fears, so threatening that she'd spilled them to Trent.

Right now her brain was too overloaded to weigh the consequences of her candor.

Trent steered her into the kitchen where he

installed a temporary bolt on the back door. Miranda still couldn't believe she had failed to activate the alarm system when she'd rushed out earlier. Then she recalled her day-long preoccupation with Trent, and wasn't surprised she'd forgotten the detail.

"I'll have George get something permanent on this tomorrow. In the meantime, gather up whatever you need for the night. You're sleeping at my place."

"I'll be fine here," she said, a stab at regaining her independence. She wouldn't be able to close her eyes anyway. Might as well get started on the cleanup.

"Humor me, hmm? If you insist on staying here, so will I." He gestured at the contents of her cupboards littering the counters and floor. "Do you honestly think either of us will be comfortable in this mess?"

He had been such a rock for her that Miranda didn't have the heart to cause him any more woe. Also, her brain was racing in a hundred different directions, trying to formulate a plan in the face of so much damage. Some distance might give her perspective. "I'll get my things."

Back in his apartment, he offered her the water bed, which she refused, and the Jacuzzi in the master bathroom, which she accepted. Her body felt as though it had been shrink-wrapped with steel wire. It would need a good bit of unwinding before sleep came.

A few minutes in the tub had her wishing for a whirlpool in her unit. Submersed in frothing water, she felt the muscle tension drain away. In its place a delicious languor stole over her. Her mind emptied of every detail but Trent . . . what he'd come to mean to her . . . what she wanted more than anything at that moment.

Miranda toweled off quickly and slipped into her aqua silk-trimmed-with-lace robe. She smiled for the first time in many hours. If the thief hadn't been so careless about scattering her clothes, she would have picked up something else, something less attractive.

At the same time she stepped from the bathroom, Trent came into his bedroom through another door. He must have showered in another bathroom because he was wearing a pair of those maddeningly sexy shorts and drying his hair. She smiled again, certain she had made the right decision.

"Sure you don't want to change your mind about my bed?"

Miranda had never been so bold. She glided over to him and draped her arms around his neck. "I want to sleep wherever you do."

He detached himself and went to work on his hair again. "I don't think that's such a good idea, Mandy."

The sharp prick of shame left her breathless. Her humiliation was complete. She had been accosted, burglarized, grilled by police, and now, rejected by Trent. A bubble of hysterical laughter welled up in her throat. What else must she endure before this nightmare ended? *I have to get out of here.* "I understand. I do."

"No, I can see that you don't." He led her to the bed and sat down beside her. "Miranda Hart, don't ever doubt that I want to sleep with you." He took one of her hands and placed it on his leg just above the knee. Then he moved it up a fraction. "Slide your hand higher and you'd know how much. But

I don't think that would do either of us any good."

Heat crawled from her fingers, branding her breasts and cheeks. Her heart took off on another roller coaster ride.

"We're both beat," he went on. "Wrung out emotionally. This isn't the time to make love, even though you think it's what you want now. Give yourself a few hours sleep and see if you still feel that way in the morning."

"It's already morning." The clock read three-thirty, and Miranda's energy level plummeted. Exhaustion overtook her like a fast train.

Trent eased her back onto the pillows and drew up the covers. He dropped a gentle kiss on her forehead and whispered in her ear, "Next time you ask, darlin', bet the ranch I'll say yes."

Miranda struggled to pull herself from the dream-shrouded abyss. Most mornings she woke instantly, but today she had to work at it. Other deviations struck her. The sun was already bright, and she hadn't slept in her own bed. Yesterday's events fast-forwarded through her memory. All in all she could not chalk it up as one of her better days.

She didn't know whether to be more disturbed about the break-in or what had taken place just before she fell asleep. Miranda had never propositioned—and there was no other word for what she'd done—a man before. Thank heaven Trent's good sense had prevailed. Embarrassment she could handle. Regret was a whole different ballgame.

Eyes closed, she lay there a few minutes longer, wondering if regret was an accurate description for what she'd be feeling this morning if Trent had shared the water bed. Somehow she doubted it.

But he hadn't, and this was a new day. Best to rise and meet it. Miranda made fast work of teeth brushing, face washing, and hair combing, then put on a jazzy purple-and-green warm-up suit that had a cheering effect on her. There were only a few hours before her flight to D.C. and in that time, she had to try salvaging enough of her wardrobe for the trip. Straightening her apartment and compiling the stolen property inventory for the police would have to wait.

Her job was more important than ever. The fabric of her life had been literally torn apart by a faceless intruder. Now she had to get to work to rebuild it.

Trent probably wasn't awake, but she didn't want to take off without letting him know her plans. When she didn't find him in the living area, she went looking in the other part of the apartment, the part she hadn't yet seen.

In the room next to his bedroom Miranda let out a gasp of surprise. It was every child's dream, an enormous space dedicated to nothing but toys and games, hundreds of them, displayed on shelves, tables, the floor. Upon closer examination she saw that none were new and some appeared to be very old. What a wonderful, whimsical hobby. But what else did she expect from a man whose favorite shirt read IT'S NEVER TOO LATE TO HAVE A HAPPY CHILDHOOD?

Miranda pushed ahead, soundlessly opening the next door. She hadn't expected this, either, a room outfitted like a dormitory. Along two parallel walls were rows of cots, neatly made up except for the one where Trent sprawled on his stomach. She tiptoed closer and called his name.

He rolled over and came up on one elbow in a single motion, squinting at her through barely opened eyelids. "Mandy?" He swiped a hand over his face. "How long have I been asleep? Ten minutes?"

His sandy morning drawl and the rasp of stubble against palm set off a sizzling chain reaction from top to toe, leaving fire storms at all points in between. Sleeping alone hadn't changed that. "Sorry to disturb you. Just wanted to tell you I'm leaving."

He sat up, yawning. The sheet fell to his waist. His chest was bare, and oh so tempting. "What's the hurry?"

It's either hurry, or throw myself on top of you. As if he'd tapped into her thoughts, Trent grinned. Miranda cleared her throat. "This is Monday. Back to business. I have to pack and go to the airport."

The grin vanished. "How can you even think of going to work today, much less leaving town? Call your office and get someone to fill in for you."

She made a disparaging sound at his order. Give a man a toehold and he stormed in to take over. "Because some thieving scum trashed my home I'm supposed to ignore my obligations? I don't work that way."

"How about working on less than four hours sleep? Can you do that?" One bare, hairy leg edged its way out from under the sheet. Tan against white was very, very distracting.

"I learned how to get by on four hours or less years ago. It's the only way you can hold down two jobs and take classes at the same time."

"The point is, you don't have to do it now." He

unfolded from the bed. Red shorts and skin, an incendiary mix. No, devastating! "You've got the damnedest superwoman complex I've ever run into. Give it a rest."

"Words of wisdom from someone who doesn't have to work for a living?" She was goading him, and they both knew it.

"Words of wisdom from someone who's been there." He came toward her, lazy grace and one hundred eighty pounds of masculinity in a formidable package. "But if that isn't a good enough reason for not going in today, try this."

Fast and sure, Trent took full claim of her lips. He kissed her once, once more, then again. Each time his mouth stayed longer, opened wider, made hers wetter.

Miranda told herself to call a halt. Instead, her fingers snagged in his hair and held him right where he was. His tongue came into her mouth then, brazen and thorough and insatiable, just the way she wanted it. The taste of him excited her, heated her blood like a shot of aged cognac.

Her palms charted his back in sinuous swirls, their touch firm at the shoulders, more delicate along his spine, firmer again at the waist.

Trent's hands echoed the motion of hers, then took a daring dip below her waist, lifting her to him. Miranda shuddered and pressed closer, obeying the ageless demand of man for woman.

"Mandy? Mandy!"

She heard her name being called as if from the mists, felt a slight shift in the alignment of Trent's body against hers.

"Make the call first."

She shrank back, appalled. She'd been drowning in that kiss, going down for the third time while Trent had been plotting. Miranda drew herself up to challenging height. "Surely you didn't expect to control me with sex."

"This isn't about control or sex. It's about what's best for you. Stop trying to be invincible for a minute and use some common sense."

She wilted a little, not caring for the implication that she was behaving unreasonably. "Why are you being so stubborn about this? It really isn't your concern."

Apparently he didn't deem that worthy of a reply. He urged her to the phone and picked up the handset. "Call Sam. Tell him what's happened. If your boss thinks you should go on with the assignment, I'll back off."

That sounded like a reasonable trade. A few minutes later, Miranda hung up. Once she had related the story, Sam didn't give her a chance to argue. "You two must be in cahoots. He ordered me to stay home not only today, but tomorrow too. How am I supposed to get any work done?"

Trent didn't bother to disguise his good cheer. "Haven't you read the statistic that you will be forty-seven percent more productive if you take time out?"

"No, I haven't. Probably because you just now made it up to suit your own purposes."

"Speaking of which," he said, snagging her wrist and pulling her back against him. "We have hours to devote to my"—he licked her lips—"purposes." His teeth closed on the bottom one. It wasn't really a bite, but it was enticing enough that her worries about work scattered like smoke in a breeze.

He could do that so easily, sweep her up in a wave of longing so intense, it made the real world a faraway illusion. She shouldn't allow herself to be overwhelmed this way. But for now, Trent had become her world. She saw only him, heard only him. Wanted only him.

Miranda sank to the bed, carrying him with her. For the first time, she took the initiative, seeking the warm haven of his mouth and the strength of his arms. Their lips fused, she began a provocative exploration of the secrets hidden behind his smile.

Her tongue glossed over the smooth surfaces of his teeth, and he gave her greater access. It made an unhurried circuit of his inner lips; he invited deeper intimacy. When it teased his tongue, Trent gave up being passive and turned the exploration into a mating dance, slow and primitive.

Miranda heard his breath come faster, harsher, and when she felt the pounding of his heart, her own quickened. A heavy drumbeat throbbed in the depths of her femininity, sending its message. *Now. Now.*

Fingers spanning his pectorals, she smoothed and kneaded, delighting in his hoarse sounds of encouragement. While one hand toyed with the patch of tawny hair, the other ventured lower. She let each fingertip have a turn at his navel, and her palm rode the wave of his swift intake of air.

He caught both her hands, halting their sensual play. "Mandy, before I'm too far gone to care, do I need to use a condom?"

Given what they were about to do, his question shouldn't have flustered her. But the intimacy of it and the bonding it represented brought her up short. Was she ready to admit that she had recently gotten a prescription for the Pill? Should she simply let Trent assume the responsibility? It couldn't hurt. Two forms of birth control were bound to be better than one.

He read her hesitation. "If you're worried about safe sex, don't. In the hospital I had every test known to modern medicine, and my family donated the blood for my surgery." He also saw her calculating that it took place over two years ago. "I haven't been with anyone since."

Miranda never thought to question his prolonged abstinence. She met his gaze and cut straight to the point. "What about the old-fashioned problem of pregnancy?"

His teeth flashed white and wicked. "Far as I know, that part of me works okay."

"Trent, be serious. This is nothing to joke about."

"No, ma'am." His tone was rife with mischief. "I get the message. Now, come here," he said, drawing her back onto the bed, bending over her. "I'll show you serious."

Miranda had never thought of herself as a sensual woman, but a hot-eyed glance from Trent could transform her in an instant. One touch, and her inhibitions dissolved. One kiss, and there was no going back. So when his lips settled on her face—at the corner of her eye, the curve of her cheek, the plane of her jaw—her whole body tingled.

The mild scrape of stubble against her neck and throat sparked a moan. He muttered an oath, knuckles chafing the side of his face. "Sorry. Didn't shave the past two days."

"No, no," she said, brushing his hand away. "I love the way it feels . . . against my skin."

This time he did the moaning. "Where do you want to feel it first? 'Cause I guarantee it's going to be on every inch of you before we're through."

The blatantly carnal promise was so close to what she wanted that Miranda had to restrain herself from tearing off all their clothes and commanding him to get on with it. But this was Trent, who never got in a hurry about anything.

She willed herself to slow down and be glad of that.

He grasped the zipper tag of her jacket. A short tug widened the opening a couple of inches. He looked down at his naked chest, then at the flesh he'd just exposed. "What do you say we even things up a bit here?" Eyes still on the tab, he waited.

"I say . . . yes." Her consent was spoken softly.

"Yes," he repeated, after sliding the zipper to her waist and discovering nothing underneath but Miranda. "Oh, yes." He skimmed the fabric off her shoulders and down her arms, baring her to his avid gaze.

For silent agonizing minutes he simply looked. Miranda held her breath the entire time. At last she felt the warmth of his hands, and let out a pent-up sigh of thanksgiving. She had waited so long.

It seemed an eternity that he lingered over her breasts, as if he would find the ultimate pleasure there. His hands conformed to the shape of them, tested their weight, stimulated her nipples, and all the while he whispered his approval against the soft upper swells. He kissed and lapped and tongue-stroked until she was writhing beneath his touch, humming with sensory awareness.

"Ah, Trent," she cried out when the sweet, enveloping suction of his mouth closed over her, greedy and giving. It was almost more than she could bear, this flood of sensations bursting at the point of contact, piercing, penetrating, until she was mindless with need. An unintelligible word escaped her lips. It sounded like a plea.

Miranda's skin was so sensitized that when he inched down her sweatpants, each pore felt the liberating touch of cool air and the enslaving power of a burning gaze.

"Oh, Mandy, do you know what seeing you like this does to me?"

She couldn't find her voice to ask what, because he had already begun working his way back up her legs. No one had ever kissed her toes or nibbled her arches. Miranda gave up trying to lie still and decided to let instinct rule her. She clutched the sheets in both hands when Trent's love bites around her ankles threw her into sensual overload. She twisted, desperate for satisfaction, and desperate for the luscious torment to continue.

"Oh!" His licking her knees while he tickled the backs of them nearly drove her over the edge into nirvana. He hadn't even touched her where it was supposed to be imperative, but it didn't matter. She was burning up from the inside out.

"You too," she urged in a throaty voice, tugging at the leg of his shorts.

He stripped them off with a flex of his thumbs and a lift of his hips.

"*This* is what you do to me." He knelt between her legs, magnificently virile and powerfully aroused. Her rapt admiration seemed to feed his desire. He wanted to be touched, and he showed her how.

Until now, Miranda had never taken time to fully appreciate the fundamental beauty and complexity of the male form. Today, with the sun shining on them, she took time. Nothing else could have been half so fascinating as having Trent Farraday all to herself.

He was such a contrast to her. Hard to soft. Angles to curves. Thrust to acceptance. She hadn't begun to get enough when he stopped her, but she understood why. His body was slick with sweat, his control unraveling.

"My turn," he ground out, pinning her hands at her sides. His mouth swooped down. Beneath them, the water bed billowed like ocean swells, at variance with the fierce undulations inside her.

Trent branded her everywhere—*everywhere*— with every part of himself. Miranda felt like a mass of swirling light and motion and energy, as if she had shed her skin and metamorphosed into a woman of wanton desires and immeasurable demands. Her every desire, he fulfilled. Each demand, he answered.

She wanted still more, and he gave her that too. They were all over the bed, reaching, striving for the elusive magic they would find in each other. Hungry, desperate sounds echoed from their lips, and she pressed hers together to quiet them.

Trent forced her mouth open. "Let it out, Mandy. Let me hear you. I want to."

She couldn't control it or stop it. Not the waves of exquisite sensations or the voice that broke free and begged, "Now, now!"

Trent had never received a gift as extravagantly generous as Miranda Hart's passion. She shimmered with it, and he shared the radiance. At the peak of her climax, he took her, and with that single stroke his own release ripped through him like a storm. Thunderous, endless, it stole his breath, his strength, and a piece of his soul.

Eight

Trent held Miranda securely during his slow reentry to awareness. He didn't open his eyes, wanting to keep the image alive in his mind of how beautiful she'd looked when she had surrendered to her pleasure. And of how he had drowned in the wonder of it. His heart seemed to swell inside him, capable of feeling more than before. Would he ever be the same now that they had made love?

He hadn't intended to rush her this way, especially after the previous night's shocks. But when she'd been so adamant about getting out of town, he knew he couldn't let her go. He'd waited too long to breach that wall of reserve.

Learning about the deprivation she had suffered and understanding how it shaped Miranda into the woman she was today filled him with hope. Trusting him with her past had opened a door to the future, providing she was willing to face up to her feelings. If only he knew what they were.

Trent didn't kid himself about his own. If he had been teetering on the brink before, her soul-baring had pushed him over. He had a bad case of loving Miranda Hart, and she was probably nowhere near ready to hear about it. That would be too big a step for her right now.

How often had she told him she had no time for romance? And yet she had crossed a barrier she'd sworn not to. That alone was significant enough to encourage him. For now, he had all the proof he needed that this was a two-way street. Of course, later on he'd need more.

Trent released a huge sigh, one of contentment rather than despair. That was the beauty of his life nowadays. He was free to dedicate himself fully to the project at hand.

For starters, he would set about introducing more fun into Miranda's fast-paced existence. Though he realized now that a deep-seated need for security drove her to maintain a killing work schedule, it didn't mean he should allow her to continue that routine. He knew that kind of obsession put Miranda on a collision course with physical and mental disaster. He had exactly what the doctor ordered, and the time it would take to convince her he was right.

Trent leaned over and planted a kiss where her neck sloped into shoulder. She smelled so good there, felt so soft. The faint moan in her throat and the way she arched her graceful neck gave him tacit approval to linger. But lingering, letting himself taste her, gave him other ideas. He eased back far enough to see her face.

Inscrutable blue-gray eyes met his. "Whatever you're feeling about this, Mandy, don't hide it from me. We're way beyond that now." He ruffled her damp bangs. "Tell me what you're thinking." To his surprise, she gave a small, tinkling laugh, almost a giggle. He'd never heard her giggle before.

"Actually, I was thinking about what popped into my head that midnight when you first showed up at my door. And how right I was."

"I can imagine," he said dryly. "You didn't exactly take one look and say, 'Here's the man of my dreams.'" She laughed again, and he loved the sound of it.

"No, I took one look at you and somehow *knew* that you knew secrets about women even I didn't, and probably shouldn't learn." A pretty blush stained her cheeks. "You're very . . . good, aren't you? At pleasing women?"

Trent couldn't believe he was blushing right along with her. Damn, she made a man feel invincible. "You give me too much credit, darlin'. Like I said, it's been a long dry spell for me. I wanted to be a real superman, stay inside you forever. But once I was, I pretty much lost control and jumped the gun."

She snuggled closer, and Trent gritted his teeth. His body had definitely made up for lost time since meeting Miranda. "I always thought men didn't, you know, go so long without sex. Over two years is a very long time."

He felt the heat from her face warm his shoulder, and couldn't figure out why she was pursuing this line. But whatever she wanted to know about him, he'd gladly tell her. "For months after the crash, I was . . . I'm not sure if I was physically unable, or just uninterested. Pain that never lets up plays hell with your sex drive. It's the last thing on your mind."

"But later, when the pain wasn't so bad . . ."

Trent shifted so he could get both arms around her. "I guess this doesn't sound macho, but the truth is, celibacy can become a habit. I got so involved in other things, so excited about the changes in my life that no woman tempted me. I didn't think much about sex."

She gave him a gentle nudge to confirm she could feel what was on his mind right then. "You're thinking about it now."

His groan was lusty, muffled against the cushion of her breast. "Now, you tempt me unmercifully."

"Good," she said, arching her back to make sure his mouth found what it was seeking. "Turnabout is fair play."

They made love, slept, shared the Jacuzzi, and made love again before wandering down to Miranda's apartment shortly before noon. She was sated and starving, and not even the sight of the havoc there diminished the glow. It was a temporary respite, she knew, but she wasn't all that eager to deal with the grim reality of her immediate future.

Working together, they restored a semblance of order to the kitchen. Then Trent started on the living room while Miranda took inventory of her refrigerator and pantry. With hunger and imagination as incentives, she might be able to come up with something close to a meal.

Twenty minutes later, she carried a tray to the low table in front of her couch. The cushions were back in place so they ate there, facing each other from opposite ends, their legs stretched out, touching.

The scene, Miranda mused, biting into a toasted bagel topped with cream cheese and smoked salmon, seemed quite domestic. Like something a lazy, loving couple might do on Sunday morning while they shared the paper.

She gulped down some guava juice to keep from choking. Such rose-colored visions spelled danger for a woman. It wasn't at all like her to romanticize an encounter based on physical attraction.

Right, Miss Sophistication. Since you do this sort of thing every day. Miranda sipped her juice more slowly. The bald truth was she had never done anything like this before, and labeling it physical attraction was the ultimate attempt at self-delusion.

She might be free to choose what she did about her feelings for Trent, but she couldn't con herself into believing they didn't exist, or that they were based on lust. Lust did not inspire a cautious woman like Miranda to confess her most guarded thoughts and fears.

Trent polished off his second bagel and reached for the bowl of peaches and blueberries she had defrosted. "I'll get hold of George as soon as I finish lunch. He can take care of the lock and send someone up to clean those mud spots off your carpet. Another couple of hours and we should have most of the mess cleared away."

He didn't seem in a rush to do whatever he normally did during the day. Or maybe he didn't do anything other than work with the kids and take off for parts unknown.

Miranda shivered as an attack of goose bumps brought back her initial impression of Trent as lacking in motivation. Still, he'd had to do something in order to own this building. Nothing about him suggested a background of inherited family wealth or privilege, though she couldn't shake the inkling of having heard his name before.

"There must be more important business you have to take care of. You needn't hang around here. I can handle this." She sounded both plaintive and defiant.

"Mandy, Mandy," he said with a shake of his head. "Taking care of you is the most important business I have." He'd kicked off his deck shoes, and his toes worked their way inside the pant leg of her sweat suit, rubbing lightly. "You are my special project. And I'm all yours."

She couldn't want him again so soon. Couldn't! The man was a demon with that soft, sexy voice, telling her he was all hers. Making her almost believe it. Miranda's hold on the bagel tightened until cream cheese oozed onto her thumb and index finger. She dropped the bagel and licked each finger in turn.

She heard the catch in Trent's breathing, but didn't brave a look at him lest he see desire burning in her eyes. "Call George," she said, knowing her hoarseness betrayed her as surely as her eyes would have.

For the next few hours, Trent directed the parade of maintenance people working to get Miranda's apartment back in shape. Dimly aware of all the activity, she concentrated on making two lists, one for the police report of stolen goods, the other to turn in to her insurance company.

Every time she discovered another item gone, every time she picked up a cherished object that had been broken, a poignant ache settled deeper inside her. To the burglar the things meant nothing beyond the few dollars fencing them would bring. To Miranda each represented a small, significant piece of her life, lost forever. She felt cast adrift, unsure of how to go about reclaiming her security.

By the time the last workman trooped out, her brooding had escalated into full-scale melancholia. Miranda almost never indulged in negative thinking. She believed a positive frame of mind increased the odds for success, as did advance planning, so she tried to stay optimistic and organized. But she hadn't been prepared for the break-in, or for what happened with Trent in the aftermath.

He came up behind her, breaking into her moody reflections. Slipping his arms around her waist, he fitted her back against his chest and nuzzled her neck. "I know just what you need about now."

"You do?" she asked turning, fearing that what she needed—far too much—was Trent. He was the problem, and he was the solution.

"Yep. You need a picnic in the park."

The orange message on his lime-green T-shirt rescued Miranda from her gloominess in a hurry. SMILE: IT'S THE SECOND BEST THING YOU CAN DO WITH YOUR MOUTH. "Have you checked the weather lately? It's been raining buckets most of the afternoon, and Brush Creek is probably overflowing." For punctuation, a rumbling thunderclap shook the windows.

He shrugged. "So? We'll be creative. Come on." He gave her arm an enthusiastic tug.

She fought him in a playful tussle all the way to the door. "Trent, you're crazy if you think I'm going to sit in the rain." When he continued pushing her along, she protested, "At least let me get my slicker."

"Nope. For my picnic, you won't need it."

"Now I know you're demented. This is crazy. We'll get soaked." She argued all the way to the garage, but he prevailed. "How do you come up with these mad ideas?"

He tucked her into the Suburban's passenger seat and kissed her complaints into silence. "My ideas? Why, from you, darlin'. You inspire me."

"I doubt if you need me to inspire ideas."

He turned somber at once. "If you believe I don't need you, Mandy, then you're missing the point of all this. Think about it."

She thought about it while he drove the few blocks to Winstead's where they ordered steakburgers and butterscotch shakes to go, and while they waited for a dripping carhop to carry out the sacks. Trent needing her was a remarkable possibility, one that both lured and frightened her.

It remained on her mind as they devoured their meal, dry and cozy inside the Suburban, at nearby Loose Park. But she forgot it temporarily when the food was gone and Trent demonstrated what he meant by being creative.

Because she hadn't dated, Miranda had bypassed many teenage diversions. Necking in a parked car, steaming up the windows, panting and petting were all gaps in her education. Trent gave her a crash course. Like everything else he'd introduced her to, she took to it immediately.

He had given her an appetite for passion, and only he could satisfy the hunger. She'd agree to anything when he swirled his tongue in her ear. His stubble on her face sent a current of wild, sensual energy jolting through her. "Trent," she said breathlessly, clutching at his shirt, "could we go all the way? Here, in the car? Now?"

"We could." He pulled her closer and let her feel that he was ready and able. "Know what I'd like even better?"

"What?" she choked out, mesmerized by the play of his fingers around, then over her nipples.

"I'd like to hold the thought and go back to your bedroom. You can't believe the fantasies I've had about that canopy bed. You and satin sheets. You wearing some of those silk things I picked up off the floor. You looking so soft and pretty and wanting me."

His fantasy was so strongly evocative, Miranda felt herself poised on the edge, about to tumble into dark velvet oblivion. "Yes. And you looking so handsome . . . and hard. Wanting me."

Trent thrust her away and twisted the key. "I won't make it if you say another word."

She didn't, and the silence during the ride was another kind of seduction. Much later, wearing only his suggestive T-shirt and a smile of satiation, she said, "So *that's* the best thing you can do with your mouth."

Wednesday morning Miranda rushed into her office, late for the first time in all the years she had worked at Callahan Associates. She averted her eyes from her coworkers, positive they would detect there the same lustrous glow she had seen in her bathroom mirror.

She hadn't meant to let Trent spend a second night in her bed; she really had made up her mind against it. But she was such a pushover when he applied his special brand of charm and persuasion. If only he hadn't applied it as her wake-up call. His deceptive lethargy had made her late.

Shaking her head in disbelief, Miranda unlocked her desk and took out a file. She had spent two whole days and nights in the constant company of a man, had talked and laughed and made love so many times she lost count. Even more inconceivable, she hadn't once thought about work or consulted her list. It was almost as if she had been acting out someone else's life. Now it was past time to get back to her own.

At the start of each morning, Miranda went over her prioritized list of all she intended to accomplish that day. She logged these short-range goals in her daily planner a week in advance. Today, because she was supposed to be conducting a seminar in Washington, she felt at loose ends.

It made no sense, she told herself, to agonize because someone had replaced her. It was a feather in her cap that her brainchild had become so successful, she'd had to recruit and train a sizable staff to meet the demand for goal-setting and motivation courses. The creation of the new department had won her a long-coveted vice presidency. If her latest proposal, the one she'd spent so long developing, was approved, Miranda hoped to gain the title of division head.

The prospect of attaining another one of her long-term goals was all it took to reactivate her sense of purpose. She dug into her proposal folder with gusto. The break from routine with Trent was illusion, not real. Excelling at work—that defined Miranda's true identity.

She worked for three hours nonstop, refusing her secretary's offer to bring her back something to eat. When she was in the office, she either didn't bother with lunch or grabbed a quick bite at her desk. Guilty about being late, she decided to forego eating as penance.

"Just as I suspected," a voice said, startling her.

Miranda's mouth opened and closed several times when she saw Trent lounging in her doorway, unannounced. "What are you doing here?" she demanded, annoyed that he had invaded her work environment. She had explained his presence at Sam's dinner as merely a neighbor doing her a favor, an eleventh hour stand-in for Walker. That excuse wouldn't wash today.

"I'm here to take you to lunch." He sounded a trifle put out, as if the answer was obvious.

"No, I don't—"

"Today you do." He sauntered over to the desk.

"—eat lunch," she finished on a determined note.

"Maybe you didn't used to, but as of now, you start." He whisked her suit jacket from its hook and held it up, taunting her like a matador with his cape.

Miranda's lips pursed, her back stiffened. "I told—"

"Oh, Miss Hart, I'm sorry." Her secretary dashed in, then pulled up when she saw Trent. "I know how you hate being interrupted. I should have locked the door." Confused, she looked back and forth between him and Miranda.

"No harm done," Trent reassured her. "I've come to see that she gets lunch. She's resisting, but the promise of food ought to take care of that, don't you think?"

"Well, I, uh—"

"See, she agrees with me. Lunch it is." He lifted Miranda from the chair and fed her resisting arms into the coat sleeves. "Stop dragging your heels,

Mandy. I'll have you back before anyone misses you. Hold her calls," he said with a wink to the stunned secretary.

Miranda seethed all the way down the corridor. Trent tried to drape his arm around her shoulders. She shook it off. "How dare you barge in like that and shanghai me?"

"Aw, come on, it wasn't quite that melodramatic." He tweaked her nose, further infuriating her. "If I had staged a genuine abduction, I'd be toting you out of here like a swashbuckler." He punched the call button and sent her a look of innocence. "Wouldn't want to embarrass you by causing a scene."

"You've already caused a scene," she said through clenched teeth. They—no, Trent had earned a number of interested stares on their march to the elevator. He had the kind of rough-and-ready good looks that drew attention like a scandal. "By the time I get back, the whole building will know." Sensing it was futile to argue, she stomped into the elevator and flattened herself against one side.

"What will the whole building know, Mandy?" he inquired pleasantly.

Her glare didn't faze him at all. "They'll know I left to go to lunch with a man."

"It wouldn't surprise me if everyone here has gone to lunch with a man at some time or another."

"No doubt." *But not one wearing a risqué T-shirt extolling the virtues of oysters to a love life. And not one who looks as though he just crawled out of bed.* "I only meant that this cannot be mistaken as business."

"Ah, I get it. Cool and refined Ms. Hart doesn't

want anybody to suspect she's hiding a lover. Bad for the image, huh? Especially when he shows up looking like this."

Lover! The word resounded inside her head like a thunderbolt. "Why are you doing this?" she hissed. "Baiting me. Calling attention to . . . to us."

He pondered awhile before replying. "I guess because you acted so damn eager to get away from me this morning." His blue-gray gaze darkened, hardened. "I got the feeling you were saying, 'Thanks for the stud service, Trent. It's been swell, but now I really must hurry back to my life.'"

Miranda flung herself into his arms, partly because he seemed genuinely hurt and partly because she bore some guilt for his feeling that way. "No, no, it wasn't like that at all." She touched his face, the beard she'd asked him not to shave. "Yes, I was anxious to get to work, but I'm always that way. It's no reflection on you. Or us."

Her claim was a jumbled mixture of truth and fiction. Because she had harbored a strong, secret yearning to stay with Trent, she'd been all the more driven to seek refuge in her job. For the first time, what she wanted was at odds with what was right for her.

"Then you're not trying to kiss me off?"

"No," she admitted, knowing she couldn't let go of Trent—not yet, anyway—no matter how often she told herself she must. It was too soon.

"So I can see you tonight, as soon as you get home?" On a roll, he added, "I'll have dinner waiting."

Miranda laughed and gave him a gentle fist in the belly. "Someday I'm going to learn how to say no to you, and mean it."

His hand spanning her belly was gentler still, warm and caressing. "By then, darlin', I hope it'll be way too late to do you any good."

Trent kept his promise. When Miranda arrived home earlier than usual that evening, she found a note on her door, telling her to change and come up to his place. Dinner was waiting. Rationalizing that she had to eat somewhere, she scrambled out of her suit, put on lemon-yellow cotton slacks and a matching sweater and made it to the fifth floor in less than fifteen minutes.

There were two places, correctly set, at the massive glass table. Candlelight and wine accompanied their Cornish game hens, wild rice stuffing, and vegetables. Trent, professing no talent for cooking, cheerfully admitted the meal came from a "Yuppie gourmet take-out joint." Miranda was feeling so mellow, she'd probably have scarfed down his infamous canned chili and asked for seconds.

That first day back on the job established a pattern for the rest of the week. Though it was never agreed on in advance, Trent appeared at her office at lunchtime. He was always well-behaved and well-dressed, as if he didn't want to give her any excuse to complain or refuse his invitation.

He had, of course, charmed her secretary, the elderly receptionist in the main lobby and every other female in the immediate area. Each successive day seemed to bring more of them out of the woodwork. Miranda's office and the lobby had never been so popular. Trent didn't flirt; indeed, he made it clear to everybody that he had his sights set on one woman only. It was immature, she supposed, but Miranda loved what his attention did for her confidence.

She was also growing accustomed to him and dinner waiting for her every night. It had been going on less than a week, and already she dreaded the time when her work would take her out of town and she wouldn't see Trent for days. Miranda had never been one to live for the moment, yet that's what she did now, ignoring what lay in the future.

She knew it had to end, and probably soon. But she had never luxuriated in an affair of the heart. Didn't almost thirty years of hard work entitle her to a few weeks of pleasure? After all, Trent wasn't monopolizing all her time. She hadn't lost sight of her goals.

By noon Friday, Miranda was in a lighthearted, almost giddy mood. Only a few more hours and she would have the whole weekend with Trent. But when he arrived, his grave expression put a damper on her high spirits. "Are you bringing bad news?" she asked, her stomach tightening. They had spent enough time together to read each other's moods. She'd never seen him looking as he did today.

"Not bad news, exactly, just something I need to show you." By rote, he went through the courtesy of helping her with the suit jacket.

With a minimum of small talk, they left the Callahan building and drove to the Plaza. Trent parked, and holding one of her hands, he picked up a brown bag in his other. They walked to the main entrance of the Board of Trade building and took an elevator to the visitor's gallery.

He motioned her to sit at one end of a bench while he claimed the other and spread out their lunch between them.

The noise from below was somewhat muted, but a palpable energy rose out of the manic atmosphere on the main floor. Electronic boards flashed prices, phones jangled incessantly, people dashed between them and the pit, men in brightly colored jackets with badges shouted and waved their hands in a ritual that made no sense to the casual observer. There was sporadic applause.

"What are they doing?" Miranda whispered, though there was no need to be that quiet.

Trent looked bemused. "Trading commodities and futures."

"Right," she said picking up her deli sandwich and munching on it. His answer was as perplexing as everything else going on around her. Trent had brought her here to make a point, she was sure. Too bad she was missing it.

"A futures contract," he explained, "is a promise between a buyer and a seller to conduct business at some point in the future at a price agreed upon today."

Miranda sipped her diet cream soda and marveled at how anyone could pretend to work within the framework of such tumult. It was like a seething snakepit, and it never let up. She pressed the burgeoning heat in her midsection, in sympathy. "How do those guys have any stomach left?"

"Some of them don't. It's called surgical removal, an occupational hazard in this business. The making and losing of fortunes exacts its pound of flesh."

Trent swept away the remains of their lunch and brought one leg over to straddle the bench. "Mandy, below you is why I never wear ties, talk fast and loud, skip lunch, or go to happy hour. I was right in the middle of the billion dollars that change hands on that floor every year. I was good at it—some said lucky—and I made a pile of money. Obscene amounts, quite legally. I could churn and burn with the best of 'em."

"I can understand why you would want to escape that pressure cooker down there." But would she be able to turn her back on the potential gold mine that went with it? "A pile of money can buy a lot of long-term security, though."

"The price is too high. Commodities futures is all supply and demand, and it's an insidious trap. Before you know it, you're wearing custom-made shirts, driving a Mercedes, showing off flashy women, chasing Scotch with antacids, and— swear to God—you never see it coming."

Once before he had spoken with contempt about the kind of man he'd been, emphasizing that he was a different person now. He didn't even go by the same name any longer. "Why am I here, Trent? What does this have to do with me?"

He reached for her hand. "It has to do with us. From this point we're going to move forward, so I wanted you to see where I've been. In time you'll know why I had to get out of this." He waved an offhand gesture at the trading floor. "And then I'll share with you where I'm going."

Miranda held her breath. By share, did he mean that he would tell her about his future plans? Or that he meant to share with her, literally? The searing pain in her stomach intensified. She mustn't let him raise the issue of anything so important. Or permanent. Commitment to a man wasn't on her list, not even as an option.

Feeling cornered, she made an elaborate show of checking her watch. "Speaking of going, I really have to get back to the office."

"In a minute. There's one more thing I want to ask you." He paused, and Miranda got the idea he was making sure to choose his words wisely. "Will you go to Disneyland with me for a week?"

Wide-eyed, she blinked several times in rapid succession. Of all the things she might have expected, an invitation to Disneyland was the last.

He smiled, the first smile she'd seen since he had entered her office over an hour ago. "It's only California, not Jupiter."

"Just like that?" She couldn't go, of course, but it didn't stop her from doing a quick mental run-through of her calendar for the next few weeks.

"No, that's why I'm asking now. To give you plenty of time to schedule vacation. You have some, don't you?"

She had over a month of accrued time, but was reluctant to tell him. A lengthy trip together was a big step, one usually reserved for couples who were seriously involved. Trent would read too much into it. "I'm not sure I'd be able to get away."

"And I'm sure it'll be no problem. All you have to do is tell Sam you're going along to chaperon the two girls from my goal-setting reward program. He wouldn't think of saying no to that. Besides, we don't leave until the school year ends."

"I'll see," she hedged, not a very decisive statement from someone used to calling her own shots. But she needed time to organize her argument.

"You might as well say yes," he said, chucking her under the chin. "Nobody, regardless of age, can resist Disney."

Nine

In the ensuing weeks Miranda found out that resisting Disney was a piece of cake compared to resisting Trent. She had once taken an assertiveness training course and learned a foolproof method for winning arguments. She picked one statement to make her point and kept repeating it, never deviating. "I cannot leave my job right now," became her mantra, and she had to restate it often.

Trent wasn't easy to convince. He had his own strategy, and once or twice she had almost given in. But before she relented, time ran out, and he and his sister left for California with the four children in tow.

Miranda ought to have been relieved that she'd withstood the pressure and stuck to her guns. Instead she felt dejected and abandoned, which made no sense at all. Not when she had achieved exactly what she'd meant to. Now she had a whole week to polish her proposal without distraction.

On Wednesday evening, Leslie called to ask if

Miranda would meet her at the hospital for a quick bite. Knowing that Les was going to reprimand her for refusing Trent's invitation didn't stop Miranda from going. For some reason, she'd lost her appetite for eating dinner alone.

"Is that all you're having?" Leslie asked, when Miranda set down her tray on one of the cafeteria's Formica tables. She had selected only a piece of cream pie and milk.

"I'm not too hungry." Mainly because her stomach had started acting up again. She chose not to mention that. "Besides, I never developed your appreciation for mystery meat." She gestured at the dark brown blob on Les's plate.

"I've eaten this so often, it actually tastes pretty good. Sort of goes with the territory." Les camouflaged the entrée with a liberal dousing of salt and pepper and steak sauce. "Have you talked to Trent since he got to California?"

Les had made it clear she could only spare about twenty minutes. Apparently she didn't intend to waste one of them on small talk. "No, I haven't heard anything."

Leslie made a disgruntled sound, but kept eating, as if waiting for Miranda to elaborate. "Nor did I expect to hear from him." Her sister's expression said *Give me a break* so eloquently, it made words unnecessary. "Well, why should he call me?"

Les washed down her food with half a glass of water. "He wouldn't have to if you'd gone along with him, like you should've."

Miranda gave up the pretense of eating her pie. "As I told him, and as I'll tell you—again—I'm in the final stages of something very important at work. I couldn't just flit off to Disneyland. Trent thinks everyone can afford to play as much as he can."

"Know what I think?" Leslie asked, spearing a limp Brussels sprout and pointing it at Miranda. "I think you stayed home because you were scared."

"Of an amusement park? Not likely."

"No, scared of what going on Trent's trip would signify. And scared you might not be a total wash-out with those kids you're trying so hard to avoid."

"Good thing you're specializing in pediatrics. You'd make a lousy psychiatrist." Miranda wondered if Les would recognize the humorous retort for the smoke screen it was.

"I don't know what spooks you worse. That you might be falling for a guy on a purely emotional level that has nothing to do with logic and lists and timetables. Or that maybe you're just as susceptible to the romantic ideal of marriage and children as any other red-blooded woman."

"I have never said I wouldn't get married," Miranda pointed out defensively. "Does the fact that I'm not in a mad rush to grab a man make me some kind of aberration? I'm simply concentrating on other priorities right now."

Leslie snorted. "Years from now you'll still be giving me the same song and dance. In the meantime your option for babies will have expired."

"Oh, puh-leeze," Miranda said, rolling her eyes. "Spare me the ticking biological clock lecture. That's one cliché I can live without ever hearing again."

"It's a cliché only because it's a fact of life. I know all about the current craze for having babies after forty. But I'll tell you, Mandy, from the medical standpoint, it's akin to playing Russian roulette."

"It doesn't apply in my case. Marriage or no, babies will never be an option for me." Her sister's incredulous gape reminded Miranda of why she had never verbalized her long-ago resolution. It was an uncommon enough stance that it required justification.

"I know you don't make decisions without a lot of thought. So why have you ruled out having kids?"

Leslie's choice of pediatrics bespoke a love of children and a reverence for family. But while Miranda understood her sister's feelings in the abstract, she couldn't identify with them. "Not everyone is cut out to be a parent. I happened to be born with a maternal gene deficiency."

"Quit trying to be amusing," Les snapped. "You're talking nonsense anyway. You practically raised me, and no one could have done it better. You'd be a terrific mother."

She started at Leslie's praise. "I'm just lucky you turned out so well. It surely didn't happen because I knew anything about child-rearing."

"Then you must have had great instincts, which is better still."

Miranda shrugged and went back to playing with the meringue on her pie. "It doesn't matter. Even if I did have the instinct and the desire, I can't take the chance."

Leslie laid down her knife and fork and leaned forward slightly. "What are you talking about? What chance?"

Miranda looked around, wishing the issue hadn't been raised in the first place. But if she didn't settle it with her sister now, she'd have to deal with it later. "The chance that something would happen to me, and I wouldn't be able to take care of a child. That I might lose all my money and not be able to provide for it. That I could be faced with bringing up my child under conditions like those we grew up in." She closed her eyes, fighting memories, fighting fears. Fighting tears. "I can't think of any act more cruel or irresponsible than condemning a child to the harshness and deprivation we suffered."

A long silence stretched out between them before Leslie asked softly, "Was our early life really so horrible to you, Mandy? Because I don't remember it that way at all."

Stunned, Miranda couldn't respond for a few seconds. When she did speak, her voice was hoarse and thick. "Les, we were dirt poor. Had nothing. Look at what happened to Mom and Dad, how young they died. It was a miserable life."

Leslie cocked her head to one side and frowned. "Well, I can't deny that we didn't have much money, but I never thought we were dirt poor. My recollections are mostly happy, that we had some good times with our parents."

Miranda's fingers gripped the edge of her tray. "How can you say that? We went through the same things, went *without* the same things."

"Maybe it depends on how important *things* are to a person. You like to surround yourself with beauty and elegance, and that suits you. I never noticed that stuff anyway, so I never missed having it and still don't.

"Then again," Less went on solemnly, "I didn't have to assume the responsibility for me. That's an awesome burden for someone no older than you were, Mandy. You had to struggle and sacrifice for a lot of years. It's bound to have left its mark. At the time, I was too young to appreciate all you were doing for me. But I do now. Someday I'll try to make it up to you."

Miranda clamped down on her lower lip to stop its quivering, wishing she could revert to being less emotional, as she had been for years. "You don't owe me a thing. I did it because I wanted to."

"No, I think you did it without even thinking. Because you didn't see that you had a choice." Leslie crossed her arms and leaned back. "But you did have a choice, Mandy. You could have abandoned me like all five of our older brothers and sisters abandoned you. Tell me they cared about what happened to either of us."

Miranda swallowed the acrid taste of bitterness. "Obviously they didn't. That was their choice. And I confess to having damned them more than once. But I've also learned that negative thinking never results in anything positive."

"Mom used to say that. Remember?"

She did remember . . . and yet Miranda had never made the connection that her mother's simple philosophy had guided her, maybe even influenced the direction of her life. "She also used to say that you can never plan the future by the past."

Leslie flashed a cherubic smile. "Think about that when you're in danger of letting old ghosts dictate your future, Mandy. They'll cheat you out of happiness every time."

Miranda analyzed that conversation many times during the following days. Could it be possible that she had fashioned a whole life based on misplaced priorities? Out of much soul-searching came the conclusion that even if she had, it was too late to start over. After all, she was happy. Wasn't she?

Miranda awaited Trent's return from California with almost shameless eagerness. She had never missed a man before and didn't like what doing so now implied.

She'd tried to program herself to believe she could have an affair. Maybe not the no-strings kind, but at least one with no *troublesome* strings. Missing Trent, lamenting her decision not to go with him, were troublesome strings.

Several months ago, she'd been so sure the excitement would wear off. It hadn't. She had expected the togetherness to grow tedious. That hadn't happened either. Instead, she relished the companionship and confidences. Laughter and lovemaking had turned out to be addictive.

On those rare occasions when she tried to foresee a future without Trent, the landscape of her life loomed bleak and barren. Reaffirming her list of goals didn't fill her with the same zeal it once had. That, more than anything, plagued Miranda during the sleepless nights apart from him.

But she couldn't let it slow her down. She was poised on the brink of real success at last. Now wasn't the time to get sidetracked. She'd begun picturing herself having the new title, along with the hefty salary increase that would accompany it. Add to that the bonuses if her division showed a profit—which she'd make sure of—and she would finally get her hands on some significant money.

Money in the bank. Plenty of it. Her lifelong dream.

So what if she spent time with Trent? She knew a number of successful women who allowed men to play a limited role in their lives. It didn't mean they were bound to them forever. Wasn't sex a basic need, like food and shelter?

Miranda assured herself repeatedly that Trent was only fulfilling that need, that her emotions weren't so involved they might endanger the quest of her ultimate goals of financial security and independence.

She wanted very, very much to believe that.

"What a long drive just to see a cabin," Miranda told Trent after he had unlocked a gate and pulled the Suburban onto a large grassy plot.

Since he had returned from California, he had stepped up his campaign to ensure that she spent almost all her nonworking hours with him. The fact that she'd refused to go on the trip didn't daunt him in the least.

"Ah, but this isn't just any old cabin." He jumped out and took off toward the small structure, motioning for her to follow.

"The operative word is old," Miranda said under her breath. She climbed down and looked around. The dwelling, towering trees, rusted iron bridge, and sluggish river at the base of the hill all looked unremarkable to her, not the stuff to prompt Trent's boyish enthusiasm. He already had the door propped open and was working on the windows.

She stepped up onto the screened-in porch, and a peek inside revealed a single room with a few rustic furnishings. "What's so special about this place?"

Trent swiped his dusty hands together. "This *place*," he said, one hand making an encompassing gesture, "is the scene of some of my best childhood memories."

Pastoral and peaceful, it was worlds removed from any of Miranda's childhood memories. "You came here often?"

"Real often when I was a kid." Hands on her

shoulders, he turned slightly and pointed. "My grandparents' farm was about three miles that way as the crow flies. It's where my mom grew up. In every direction, there were tons of her relatives."

Miranda closed her eyes and traveled back in time. "When I was very young, I used to create escapist fantasies. In them, my grandparents lived on a farm where there were hordes of animals, all kinds. And I had my own pony. Her name was Lady Jane—silly name for a pony, I guess—and I could ride her anytime I wanted. Only me."

The hands that had been resting lightly on her shoulders dug in. "Did you ever get to ride a pony, Mandy?" Trent's voice had grown as tight as her muscles.

She pivoted and gave him a cheery smile. "No, but I've contacted a stable about riding lessons. It's inching up to the top of my list."

"I've heard that word more than once, from both you and Les. Is there really a list?"

Miranda gawked at him until she remembered that not everyone subscribed to her methods. "Lists, plural." She held up her index finger. "There's the big one, my master plan, if you will. That includes all the major goals I want to accomplish over the long term."

Miranda raised the middle finger. "The next list is corollary, composed of intermediate steps that will advance me to my primary goals. Then there are—"

He captured her ring finger and brought it to his mouth before she could say, "tertiary." After the bath from his tongue, she had a hard time saying anything.

"All that talk about goals reminded me of my primary one—to kiss you as often as possible."

Hands shaping her face, he bent to touch her mouth with his.

Warmth flowed through Miranda like the rippling water below. She swayed against Trent, a motion as unhurried and gentle as the wind whispering through oak leaves high above them. Their kiss transcended a mere physical joining of lips. Miranda felt a fundamental link with Trent and her surroundings and the mood, a connection that defied words.

"Whew," he said, breaking the contact to look into her eyes. "Either I am one heck of an achiever, or you used some kind of power play on that kiss."

Pleased that he'd felt the mystical union, too, her lips curved in an enigmatic smile. "Let's just say I believe a man who pursues his goal diligently should be rewarded."

"I will remind you of that often." He laced their fingers together, and they set off on the grand tour. Acorns from a stately black oak crackled beneath their footsteps while a woodpecker played counterpoint on a nearby maple.

Trent halted at a rock-ringed firepit, propping one foot on a stone. "We fried a ton of fish here. Cousin Albert was the expert at catching them, then we'd cook them over an open fire in a huge iron kettle. Uncle Will always stretched out in that hammock, pestering the cooks.

"All around there'd be washtubs of drinks on ice, and inside the cabin, every table would be loaded down with potluck dishes everyone had brought. To my mother's family, there was no such thing as too many reunions, and what's a reunion without mass quantities of food?"

"She's upholding tradition well." When Trent had insisted that Miranda meet his parents and grandparents, plus a host of other kin at a similar gathering, she'd protested. All her life she had avoided such encounters.

His will proved stronger, and once over her initial anxiety, she had enjoyed the Fourth-of-July backyard picnic. His family had been exceptionally warm and welcoming. "I couldn't believe all those people bearing all that food."

"And they couldn't believe I showed up bearing such a fine-looking woman, 'with brains yet, praise the saints,' to quote Aunt Lena."

Miranda laughed and bent to pick up an acorn that the elements had buffed to a shine. "She came right out and asked me what my intentions were toward you."

Trent rolled his eyes and shook his head. "Subtle, she's not. Count yourself lucky if she didn't ask anything truly personal."

"Well, the fact that we live 'in each other's hip pockets' definitely interested her. She commented several times on how handy that must be."

"I'll bet. Lena isn't vicious or mean-spirited, but she does love to snoop, especially if she sniffs romance. Knowing you, she didn't get much satisfaction." He resumed walking, heading for the steep bank overhanging the water.

"I told her the truth. That I'm a tenant in your building and that we're friends."

"Right. Lena probably fell for that hook, line, and sinker. Especially the 'friends' part."

Did he expect her to advertise the news that they were lovers? That was not a subject Miranda cared to discuss. Getting on with the tour made more sense. "Let me guess. The old swimming hole," she said, indicating a pocket formed by a slight bend in the river.

"You got it. If there were a lot of us, the bigger ones would hoist someone smaller on their shoulders and we'd have jousting matches, hand to hand to see who toppled over first. The year my brother got his height, before he discovered girls and had to be cool, nobody could beat us."

He spoke of those times with such fond remembrance that Miranda got caught up in vicarious nostalgia. The idealistic fantasies of her youth had focused on places and things she coveted. Trent was describing something less tangible. "It isn't the place that was special," she said in a hushed voice. "The people and the togetherness you shared, those are the important parts of your memories."

"Of course." To her it had been a discovery; to him, a truism. "In the end, that's all any of us can count on."

"Another school of thought says you can't count on anyone except yourself." Miranda had lived most of her life believing that. Because of their disparate backgrounds, she and Trent were doomed to disagree on this issue.

Rather than argue, he brushed her lips with a kiss. "Trust can be learned, Mandy, if you put your mind to it. It's like any other goal you aim for."

In an eyeblink, he shed his grave expression for a grin. "Now, come on. Let's see if I can still find the hidden trail down to the waterin' hole."

As they slipped and slid their way down the sheer embankment, Trent filled her full of tall tales about cowboys chasing bank robbers, jungle mercenaries fighting evil dictators, and alien invaders out to colonize planet Earth, all adventures he and his relatives had acted out as children. "I wonder if what and how you play determines the sort of person you grow up to be," Miranda wondered.

"I'm sure it does. That's why I work so hard at getting my kids to play." He jumped off the bottom terrace and turned to give her a hand. "You'd be surprised at how many don't know how to."

"No, I wouldn't be a bit surprised." At thirty, she still didn't know how.

The bank was rocky with everything from gravel to boulders large enough to sit on. Miranda settled on one and watched Trent skip smooth, flat stones until he challenged her to a contest.

After he taught her how, they battled to a draw. Then they took a hike around the bend for a short lecture on river geography. Here, water less than six inches deep burbled its way through the shallows. Trent and Miranda claimed separate rocks, at right angles to each other, knees almost touching.

"This part of the bank is sandy. Did you ever camp out down here?"

"Only once," Trent said, staring down at his hands. "The relatives used it mostly for day gatherings, but the summer we were sixteen, Sean and I convinced our folks that we were brave enough and responsible enough to stay overnight. Sort of a male rite of passage, I guess."

"Sean? Another cousin?" She'd met Trent's brother and several cousins at his parents' house, but none named Sean.

He didn't reply for a long time. When he did, his voice sounded thin, as if it had traveled over a great distance. "Sean was my best friend, since before I can remember. He was brilliant and generous and fun. Everybody loved him."

Miranda felt storm clouds approaching and

looked up. Above was nothing but bright, crystalline blue. Then she realized her wariness had been triggered by a storm within Trent. His hands shook visibly. His eyes were fixed on some remote horizon.

"He was a genius when it came to computers, kind of like he really understood them, not as machines, but as kindred spirits. Companies were after him all the time. He could ask for and get just about any amount of money."

Miranda noticed his use of the past tense. "Then you were both doing well financially?"

"Oh, yeah. Raking it in." He clamped one hand over the other. It didn't halt the tremors. "The difference between us was that he spent all his free time doing volunteer work in the inner city. Finally, he said he had more money than he'd ever need, so he quit the fancy job and dedicated himself to his community center project."

And now Trent was doing the same thing. "So he's the one who got you involved in that kind of work?"

He flinched, as if she'd struck him. "You want to hear something funny? I wouldn't even go down there with him. Couldn't imagine there being anything in that place to interest an upwardly mobile guy like Tom Farraday."

Miranda squirmed, disturbed by the words that until recently would have described her too. "But you went." Just as she had.

"Not until too damn late!"

She had never heard Trent shout. Never. Dense summer air supported the harsh sound, intensifying its impact. "What happened?" she whispered, weighted down by dread.

"Sean had met a woman. Tessa. They used to laugh and say they were two old souls who'd been together many times before. I could almost buy it. They thought alike, believed in the same causes, wanted the same things. Most of the time that doesn't work, but for them, it did."

He picked up a baseball-size stone and with a mighty heave, sent it crashing to the opposite shore. Miranda blanched at the sudden violence, sensing it substitute for some stronger emotion.

"Tessa wanted to get married at her family's church in Dallas. I was going to be best man. Sean and I were flying down there together, a few days before the wedding."

Trent's eyes were wild with a haunted, hunted look. "The plane crashed just before landing. Wind shear, they said. I survived. Sean didn't."

"Oh, no," she breathed, moving to kneel before him. "Oh, Trent." Such inadequate words of comfort, and yet the only ones that came out. She was leading with her heart, not her intellect. Feeling, not thinking.

Miranda stared into his eyes, but they didn't see her. They were frozen on a Texas runway, more than two years in the past. She remembered. He'd made the local papers and business journals. *Kansas City wunderkind narrowly escapes death. Tom Farraday's uncanny luck continues in Dallas . . .*

"I'd downed a couple of drinks on the flight, and we got into . . . a heated discussion, I guess you'd say. Sean spent most of the trip arguing that I was wasting my life and jeopardizing my health, chasing something I didn't need, or even like all that much."

"You were only doing what you thought you had to," she said, defending herself as much as the exiled Tom.

"No, I was too pigheaded to see it, but Sean had hit the bull's-eye. I was making all the right moves and not getting one minute's satisfaction from any of it."

Teeth bared, Trent let his head fall back. Deep grooves etched his eyes and mouth, as if he were still suffering the pain. Miranda folded her arms around him, aching to give solace when she feared there was none. His chest pumped in and out like a bellows as he fought to contain the emotion.

"The irony is that Sean had every reason to live, and if there were any justice, he would have. While I—"

"No!" Her fingers silenced his self-condemning words. "Don't say that. It's not true."

Miranda understood it all now. Why Trent had turned his back on a high-paying career and why he had to do the youth work. It showed her everything she needed to know about the man— his character, loyalty, and dedication.

It also solved the mystery of why Trent Farraday had been different from the start, why she couldn't dismiss him. In her heart of hearts she had known that he possessed all the best qualities a woman searched for in a man to love.

She did love him. It came to her so clear and true that Miranda didn't even try to argue against the futility of such a love or to doubt its rightness. It existed, one of life's inevitabilities. Like Trent's misery.

She wanted to say so much, but there were no words. She ached to do something to ease his burden. At that moment, she would have given up everything she owned to spare him this suffering, but she knew it wouldn't be enough.

So she held him, and wept the tears he wouldn't allow himself to shed.

Ten

When Miranda and Trent at last climbed back up the hill, she stepped on level ground a different woman. Like a baptism, the incident at the river's edge had transformed her. After months of wavering, confronting the truth was like having a great weight lifted from her.

Trent's outpouring had seemingly relieved him of a similar load. Miranda suspected that he had never before voiced his feelings about Sean's death and the profound change it had effected on his life.

Earlier she had questioned the necessity of a two-hour drive to this remote spot. Even Trent probably couldn't have guessed it would turn out the way it had. Miranda was not the superstitious sort, but she believed their pilgrimage here had been fated.

It had given Trent a chance to exorcise his ghosts. And it had shown her that by denying love, she had allowed limiting forces to rule her. Accepting love would restore balance to her life and free her to get on with her plans.

"I can tell you're grappling with something heavy," he said. "I've seen a dozen different looks across you face since . . ." His head dipped in the direction of the water.

"That's because I've realized at least a dozen different things. I'm glad you trusted me enough to . . ." Her head tipped, repeating his gesture. Saying more would be superfluous. They were communing silently.

"Down there, when you were holding me like you'd never let go, I heard you speaking without words. Right away, I felt better. I understood that I'd been spared for a reason. I had been telling myself that intellectually, but today I felt it in my heart. I have a lot to live for."

"Yes!" Miranda said a silent prayer of thanks. Her message had reached him. "You can make sure Sean's work goes on. And you have—"

"You." He grasped her upper arms and looked deeply into her eyes. "I love you, Mandy. Finding you has given me everything I need. You're my center."

"Oh, Trent." Awash with emotion, Miranda could say nothing else. It was almost too much to assimilate at once. That she loved him was easy to admit to herself now. But she hadn't had time to consider he might love her as well.

"There was something else going on down there, but it didn't come across as clearly. Like the signals were mixed."

Extraordinary. "After you'd told me about Sean, I wanted to make love to you. It was the only thing I could think of to give, when I desperately needed to give." Her fingers picked at the braided sash of her jumpsuit. "But it seemed out of place and inappropriate, like a violation of his memory."

Trent's smile went through many variations, but, oh, she loved that sweet, hesitant one best of all. "I think Sean would see it as the very finest way to affirm life," he said in a husky voice. The smile broke through again, stronger this time. "And so do I."

Because Miranda now understood and accepted her love for Trent, she could show it without shyness or uncertainty. "I didn't see a bed in the cabin."

"Mmm," he agreed, fitting his hands to her waist to begin a seductive kneading. "And we both know what chiggers can do when bare skin meets grass. They're so voracious. Come to think of it, I'm starting to feel that way myself."

His teeth found the sensitive skin on her nape and began a gentle feasting. A low purring sound came from Miranda's throat. It was always this way between them, this instant attunement. Trent had quickly discovered every pleasure point on her body, and he knew instinctively how to touch them.

"We could try the backseat," he murmured in her ear, each word followed by a flick of his tongue.

Miranda's breath flowed out on a sigh. He had such a magical way with her ears. She slipped off one sandal, hooking her leg behind his calf to bring them into a closer melding. "Last time, you said your back couldn't stand that again. Too hard."

"Too hard is right." He rocked his hips against hers. Miranda absorbed the motion, glorying in the potent, masculine response she had drawn from him.

Her lips tingled, and she couldn't wait any longer. Her tongue moistened a curve on his neck just below where the beard stopped. Then along his cheekbones above it. "You taste so good. All over, but especially here." She sampled his mouth at leisure, inside and out, quivering when his nimble tongue initiated its own lazy, erotic coupling.

They had made love many times, in different places, in many ways. Miranda marveled at their talent for making each time seem better, in a different way. Or did lovemaking become increasingly richer when strengthened by the ties of love? Perhaps that was the real miracle.

He leaned back, his gaze playing over her like a lambent flame, tempting her to test the fire. "Want to be daring?"

She followed his over-the-shoulder glance. "Uncle Will's hammock? That is daring. Something tells me it wasn't designed for what we have in mind, especially with your back."

He grinned a lusty pirate's leer. "We'll never know unless we try. If it doesn't work, the ground isn't far and the grass is soft. I'm willing to take my chances with the chiggers."

He took her mouth again, his silky, evocative claim a luscious portent of what would follow. Matching each languid thrust of his tongue into her mouth with a slow back step, he drew them toward their destination. His palms shaped her bottom, pressing soft against hard, causing her to tremble and him to shudder.

When she felt the hammock behind her, she reached out to the nearby tree to steady herself. She held on to it, breathlessly watching while Trent's tanned fingers freed the buttons of her jumpsuit. He peeled it off her shoulders and let the bodice drop to her waist.

"These things," he said, stroking the flesh-colored lace trim on her pink silk bra, "are made to drive a man crazy." His lips traced the scalloped edging before nudging aside the straps to nibble at her shoulders. "Unfasten it for me, Mandy."

She grasped the front closure, then taunted, "Not until you shirt disappears." It was another oyster bar T-shirt that said SHUCK ME, SUCK ME, EAT ME RAW.

"Done." He stripped it off in a flash, flinging it to the ground. "Your turn."

A faint click sounded as Miranda met his challenge, dropping the silken wisp onto his shirt. He growled, and she stepped back, shaken by his very primal response to her bare breasts. "That day when we were eating chicken, you told me you were a breast man."

"Did I lie?" His hands cupped the twin weights, cherishing. "I love all of you, Mandy. This." He kissed the valley formed by the swelling flesh his hands framed. "And this." His fingers strummed her nipples into hard peaks, while he watched her desire build and listened to her small whimpers of encouragement.

He crossed his arms behind her, bringing her closer. "But this is best, you next to me." He felt hot and sleek, the rough texture of him deliciously abrasive against her skin. Miranda twisted and writhed, unable to get close enough to assuage the fire consuming her.

His hands ventured lower, spanning the dip at her waist, then over the lusher curves of her hips and lower, sweeping away the jumpsuit and her panties so she could step free of them and her sandals.

By the time he had kissed and caressed his way

back up, Miranda's legs were in danger of giving way. Trent was a master at slow loving.

She wasn't half as smooth when she went to work on the buttons of his jeans. Her fingers barely functioned, and her breath rushed out in shallow puffs. But he didn't seem to notice, because when she freed him and knelt to begin the same electrifying ascent of hands and mouth, his breath was just as shallow, and his fingers in her hair just as shaky.

His raspy voice stroked like an inflaming touch. "If you don't want tree bark imprint on your back, I'd better see if I can master this thing." He steadied the hammock and gracefully stretched out on his back. "I've never lain naked in here before. I feel like a satyr."

Miranda looked him all over, from the wicked glint in his eyes, to the tantalizing fan of hair on his chest, and the lavish display of masculine arousal. She loved it all. A sudden rush of heat touched off an answering surge of blood through her body. "You *look* like a satyr. Scandalous and debauched."

"Then come here, nymph," he teased, grabbing her hand. "Let's get on with the ravishing."

With great care, Miranda eased herself down along his length, levering her upper body slightly away. The swing of the hammock made her feel as though she were sailing over calm waters. She smiled at the fanciful analogy. The journey wouldn't stay calm for long. Not with Trent playing his enticing games on the nerves of her spine.

"The sun does beautiful things to you, your eyes, your skin, your breasts. Look."

She couldn't. Couldn't tear her gaze away from the wonder in Trent's eyes as he watched her. But she could feel, and she knew that his admiration, not the sun, had made her dreamy-eyed, made her skin misty with desire, made her breasts flushed and heavy with the need to be taken into his mouth.

"Give them to me."

Miranda arched her neck, bending back as he leaned upward. "Aaah," she cried out, so exquisite was his strong pull on her nipples. One, then the other, back and forth, drawing them, drawing her, until she could not hold back the tidal wave of inner spasms cresting in the center of her femininity. "Trent? Trent!"

"I'm here. I've got you." He brought her to rest fully atop him, kissing and nuzzling her into quiescence. But the hammock's motion kept the aftershocks alive.

"How do you do that to me?" she choked out. "So fast. So easy. I never would have believed I could turn into a wanton. You are a bad influence."

"Yeah. Just what you've been needing, *baad* company." He enticed her with only a nudge of his hips. "Can you feel what bad shape I'm in?"

Miranda shifted and reached between them to measure him with a bold hand. "Bad? No way. But I think I know how to make you feel *sooo* much better."

Teeth clenched, Trent let out a hiss of gratification as he watched Miranda take him into her. His fingers reached up to latch onto the dowel, and Miranda fit her palms against his. The dip and sway of the hammock ruled out vigorous activity, but the restraint made their joining all the more intense. Signals sent with inner muscles, eye contact, and heartfelt emotions rivaled the power of their most heated lovemaking.

Passion ensnared them in its gossamer strands, uniting them in such complete consonance that they moved as one, thought as one, became one. Miranda was so awed by the absolute perfection of it, her eyes filled.

"Tell me, Mandy! Say it!"

"I . . . love you. I love you, Trent." The tempest raging inside her demanded release, and she abandoned herself to it and to the only man she'd ever loved.

Trent followed Miranda into the farthest reaches of ecstasy, pledging everything he had, everything he was. "Never stop saying it, Mandy. Never, never, never."

She didn't want to do this.

Miranda never suffered from stage fright. Until today. Driving back from their trip to the cabin yesterday, Trent had reminded her of her promise to speak to a group of children at the community center. Weeks ago, in a moment of weakness, she had agreed to do it, mainly because he'd made her feel guilty for refusing to go to Disneyland.

Trent was talking to the group now, introducing her. There were less than twenty, all under twelve, including Bird. They didn't look threatening, but her insides were coiled in knots. What uplifting message could she use to motivate, when the odds were slim that any of them would ever escape and succeed? How well she understood that hopelessness.

Then she remembered Sam. Suppose he'd had Miranda's attitude. He would never have bothered to come to her school, never given her the courage and inspiration to try for a better life. And there was Trent, who could have reveled in his wealth, but had chosen instead to give generously of himself and his money. Didn't she owe her best to the two men who had influenced her so much?

Squaring her shoulders, she drew a deep breath and walked briskly to the front of the room to take command of her audience. *Smile. Make eye contact. Speak positively, and tell them something important. Something to remember.*

"Once upon a time there was a little girl named Miranda. She lived not far from here . . ."

Miranda talked for thirty minutes, and held nothing back. She'd made an on-the-spot decision to be completely up-front about her background. She didn't know how she was able to do it or why she needed to. But she did know that nothing else would be good enough. If she could make an impact on those listening, as Sam had done for her, it would be worth the price she paid for her candor.

Oddly enough, confession didn't turn out to be nearly as painful as Miranda had always feared. For years she'd guarded her past like a secret guilt. Did hoarding the hurts somehow magnify their significance? Had she, as Leslie charged, allowed old ghosts to dictate her future?

By the time she finished, she could tell that her eagerness, her absolute faith in the power of goal setting and self-motivation had transferred itself to the group. She'd seen it happen too often to mistake the signs. The room pulsed with an energy that hadn't been present before.

His eyes shining with pride and satisfaction, Trent led the applause. Miranda was a little embarrassed by its enthusiasm and duration, but oh, so pleased. She was used to appreciative audiences, but the buoyancy she felt now went beyond the usual thrill over a job well-done.

Many of the youngsters mobbed her, vying for attention to ask questions. To ask advice. She was in her element, and her satisfaction soared to new heights.

Bird lingered as most of the others drifted over to the refreshment table. "That was just outstanding, Miranda. You had everyone really paying attention. That's kind of hard to do with some of these characters."

"Thank you. It did go well, didn't it?"

"The best program we've ever had." Bird hesitated for a time, as if reluctant to leave.

"Is there anything you want to ask?" Miranda prompted.

"Are you and Trent going to get married soon?"

The question sent Miranda reeling. Even though she and Trent were in love, she refused to think about the *M* word.

"N-no, Bird," she stammered. "Why would you think so?"

Bird wound a tiny finger in her blond curls. "Well, he must like you a lot, to invite you here. And *everybody* loves Trent. Miss Kelly, that nurse who comes to the clinic, tries her best to flirt with him, and he's never asked her to go anywhere."

What an astounding assumption to make based on the evidence. "Just because Trent isn't interested in Miss Kelly doesn't automatically mean he wants to marry me."

With absolute conviction, Bird said, "Remember what you said about deciding what will make you happy, then working very hard to get it?" At Miranda's nod, she continued, "If I were a woman,

I'd work for all the things you have. And then I'd work to have Trent too. Forever."

Out of the mouths of babes. Was it even remotely possible that she could accomplish everything on her list, and have Trent too? Forever?

Much later, when the crowd had cleared out and she was alone with Trent, he said, "I know this is what you do, Mandy, but I didn't realize just how good you are at it. That was some show. Those kids left here flying high."

His praise warmed her. "That's the idea. You have to get them really fired up, so the fervor will sustain itself and be transformed into action."

He snagged her around the waist with one arm, drawing her close. "My fervor is at an all-time high. Let's go home and transform it into action."

The next morning Trent left her apartment shortly after dawn. He was taking off on another one of his mysterious trips. But this time, he'd told her the secrecy concerned a surprise he would be springing on her soon. There had been few surprises in Miranda's adult life. She preferred it that way.

Rather than second-guessing his secret, Miranda went to work bright and early. Flushed with yesterday's triumph, she could feel a burst of productivity in store. She had a whole week to burn the midnight oil, and next Monday, she would present her proposal to Sam. Within a month, she could be exactly where she'd worked so hard to get.

Her life was . . . almost perfect.

It didn't last.

On Friday, Miranda dragged herself home, exhausted and barely able to stand. She had put in sixteen-hour workdays, and all-night battles with insomnia had turned her into a zombie. Tonight she was running on empty.

Shedding her clothes, she shrugged into a kimono and staggered to bed. Feeling wretched and alone, she wished Trent were there to hold and comfort her.

On the other hand, she was relieved that he wasn't. What if she became violently ill again, as she had been for the past two nights? She couldn't bear the thought of his seeing her so sick and helpless. Better that he not return until tomorrow. She'd be back to normal then.

Miranda awoke shortly after midnight and barely made it to the bathroom. The symptoms were far worse tonight than before, and frightening. As soon as they subsided, she called her sister at the hospital and described them.

"You can't tell me this just happened tonight," Leslie nagged. "Why have you waited so long to tell me?"

"Les, please," Miranda begged. "I'm scared. Tell me what I should do."

"Get Trent to drive you down here ASAP. Come to the emergency room and have them page me."

Miranda bit back the irrational urge to burst into tears. She gripped the phone cord. "Les, I can't go into the hospital. I can't! I don't have time."

"Mandy, this sounds like an ulcer, and that is not something to play around with. Get your butt down here in fifteen minutes or I will be calling Trent to ask why."

Miranda broke the connection. She hadn't told Les that Trent was out of town, knowing her sister would send an ambulance. If she had to make a trip to the hospital, Miranda was determined it would not be done amid sirens and flashing lights. But she was afraid a cab would take too long to get there. What if she had another attack?

The only alternative was to drive herself. And hope she made it.

Eleven

Miranda's hospital room door swept open for what seemed like the hundredth time that day. "This place is busier than the airport on Thanksgiving weekend," she grumbled, not expecting sympathy. That was in short supply around here.

"Aha!" Leslie announced. "Diagnosis—improving patient syndrome. She's starting to complain."

"I have put up with poking and probing and never-ending tests. I'm entitled to be grumpy. Now, when can I leave?"

Assuming nursing duty, Leslie came over to the bedside and removed Miranda's IV, chucking it into the wastebasket. "They're doing the paper-work now. As soon as Dr. Walden stops by for a final chat, you're free."

"What a relief." Miranda sat up and swung her legs over the side of the bed, intent on getting dressed. Her head started spinning, and she inhaled sharply.

"Take it easy," Les advised, grabbing her arm. "You're not ready to go ten rounds yet."

"How can two nights in here make me so weak?" She got down, determined to walk to the closet for her clothes.

"It's not the two nights in here, you ninny. Burning the candle at both ends for years got you in this fix. I'm sure Dr. Walden will tell you the same thing."

"No doubt," Miranda said wryly. "If he doesn't, he'll be the first one who hasn't." Only Trent, who'd been to see her several times a day, had refrained from giving advice. He'd just held her hand and told her funny stories. That had made her feel better than any medicine.

Dr. Walden came in then. With Leslie witnessing, he discussed the treatment for ulcers. He issued orders concerning diet, medication and, at length, the necessity of changing her lifestyle to reduce stress.

"But, Doctor," she protested, "everyone I know is stressed out. There are so many pressures."

"Your sister told me about your job. Use that talent to set alternative goals that will be less stressful."

He made it sound easy. "You don't understand. . . ."

"What I understand, young lady, is that if you choose not to take my advice—and it is your choice—I've no doubt you'll be an excellent candidate for surgery within months."

With typical brusqueness, he strode from the room, letting his parting words ring in Miranda's ears for a long time. What a mess! And what was she going to do about it?

She turned it over and over while getting dressed. It would be hard to change, but she didn't care for the other option. Bowing to policy, she accepted the wheelchair ride down to where Trent was waiting to pick her up. From start to end, hospitalization had been a demoralizing experience she never wanted to repeat. Especially not for surgery.

"Hang on," Trent said as soon as he had her buckled into the seat. "I'll have you home before you know it."

Miranda had never seen him look so grave. Strain had transformed his usual laugh lines into deeper grooves. He had suffered as much as she, though in stoic silence. That had taught her yet another lesson about love. She'd never believed she was selfish, but against everyone's advice, she had disregarded her symptoms for months. Her negligence had ended up hurting Trent, as well as herself.

Starting today, she was going to make up for that. She would pay attention to those who cared about her and try to slow down. Surely she could figure out some way to do that.

"Just getting out of there has made me feel a hundred percent better," she told him as they pulled out of the driveway. "Do we have to go straight home? It's such a gorgeous day. Why don't we take a walk in the park?"

His grip on the wheel tightened. "You were very sick, and you're still weak. It's better if you rest."

"For three days, people have been offering suggestions about what's best for me. I had to listen. But right now, a milk shake and a walk in the park are just what I need."

She saw his argument forming and cut him off. "I promise to creep along like a snail and not overdo it. But I really need to be outside and breathe fresh air. Please?"

He looked her over, as if making his own diagnosis. "All right. Just for a little while." He stopped by Winstead's for the shake, then drove on to Loose Park.

They strolled a short distance and claimed a bench near the Jacob Loose statue. Miranda sipped her cold, creamy shake and practiced relaxing. "I've started a new list. Ways to combat stress in my routine. I'm going to spend an hour in the park every day, winter and summer."

"I've never known anyone who had to make a list to enjoy a simple pleasure. Aren't you defeating the purpose when you make it just one more goal you have to attain?"

His rebuke depressed her. "Well, I've got to start somewhere. At least I'm trying."

He turned to her. "This isn't the time or place or way I wanted to tell you about my surprise. But after what's happened, I don't think it's a good idea to put it off."

He looked very tense. "I thought surprises were happy.

"Yeah," he said, sighing. "Let's hope so. Miranda, I've been running back and forth to North Carolina because I've had a project in the works there. It's almost finished, and when it is, I want you to move there with me."

"Move! To North Carolina?" she squeaked, almost dropping her cup. Surprise was too mild a word. "Why?"

"Years ago, when I was looking for things to do with my money, I bought a run-down estate at a foreclosure auction. I hadn't a clue as to what I'd do with it, but I picked it up for a song. Early last year, I began renovations."

"You're going to live on an estate in North Carolina, and you want me to go too? Whatever would we do there?"

"Originally, my plan was to convert it into a youth camp where I could handle up to a hundred disadvantaged kids at a time. It's beautiful there in the mountains."

Trent and hundreds of children? Miranda swallowed against the sudden queasiness in her stomach. "What role do I play? Children aren't my field."

"When I knew I'd fallen in love with you, I expanded the concept. The property covers acres. Separate from the camp, we can build a retreat type facility for motivation and goal-setting seminars." His features became animated. "You wouldn't have to travel because people could come to you. And it'd be all yours, anything you wanted to do."

In three sentences he had condensed the essence of the proposal she would be presenting to Sam. But she couldn't even consider implementing it with Trent because of her commitment to Sam.

Miranda jumped up and took off on one of the jogging paths. Her mind was racing, and she needed physical activity to balance it. Her life was crumbling around her, and she had no contingency plan to halt the destruction.

"What do you think of my idea?" he asked, falling into step beside her. "It'll take a while to get your facility designed and built, but I didn't want to start without you."

"I . . . it sounds like a great idea." *But not for me.*

"Mandy, slow down and stop acting spooked. This is our future. Look at me and let's talk about it."

She stopped, propping her hands on the back of a bench near the lake. Her breath was coming fast as if she'd jogged the entire loop. "The future you described might be yours, but it can't be mine. Even if I wanted to go there and be with you, I can't leave here. Not ever."

"Wait a minute. Aren't you the person who's always saying you can do anything if you want to badly enough? Don't you want to be with me?"

Miranda blinked back the moisture veiling her eyes. "It isn't fair, you know, springing this on me, expecting me to give up everything, leave it all behind and chase after you like a camp follower."

"Whoa," Trent said with a shaky laugh. "Maybe I got the cart before the horse. First things first, will you marry me? Then we'll go to North Carolina, where we'll each do what makes us happy, and while we're at it, maybe we can make a baby, or two, of our own. Oh, hell. This isn't the way I intended to propose either. I had a much more impressive scenario worked out."

She sniffed. "You don't understand. The answer wouldn't change regardless. I can't go anywhere. By extension, no marriage. No babies."

Trent lay both hands on her shoulders. "That's it? You're saying there can be no *us* because you can never leave Kansas City?"

"That's it."

"Miranda, I'm trying to be real patient here, but you damn sure have to give me a better reason than that. The only family tie you have here is Les, and she's already decided to go West once she's completed her residency."

"It's Sam," she said starkly.

He gave her a little shake. "You're supposed to

love me, yet you refuse to go because of another man?"

Might as well spread all the cards on the table. "When I was sixteen, Sam came to speak to my class. He told us about his background—it was as dismal as mine—and how he'd overcome it and succeeded. It was as if his words were for me alone. I knew right then where I wanted to go, and that I needed an education to get there."

She paused to watch a radio-controlled toy boat skim the lake's surface. "Anyway, a few weeks later I scraped together my courage and bus fare and rode to his office. Of course, they weren't going to let me see him, but I just kept repeating, 'I have to talk to Mr. Callahan.' Finally, they could see I wasn't going to give up, and I got in."

"You had plenty of guts, even then."

"I had nothing to lose. I asked—begged, really— for him to find me a job that day. I raised my hand and swore that if he gave me an opportunity to work my way through college, I would stay with Callahan Associates for the rest of my life, and that I'd be the best employee in history."

She crossed her arms, withdrawing, steeling herself. "I will never willfully break that promise to Sam, not with all I owe him."

"Sam Callahan isn't the devil, Miranda, and you're not Faust. You didn't sell your soul."

"As I said, you don't understand."

"All I understand is that you're saying your job is more important than our love and being together and having a family. That tears me up, but what can I do to fight it?"

They walked back to the car without exchanging a word, and rode back to the apartment the same way. The distance between them could not have been greater had Trent already gone to North Carolina and left her behind.

To Miranda, it seemed that he had accepted the finality of her decision without much of a fight. So, what did she expect? What did she want? For him to lose his temper and rant at her? Cause a scene? No, that was crazy.

He did none of those things, but he hadn't given up. Over the next week he came at her from different directions with different arguments each time they were together. It was a nonviolent war of persuasion, and Miranda had only one defense— her pledge to Sam.

Finally, Trent fielded the ultimate weapon. "I am leaving for North Carolina tomorrow. If you decide to put that agile brain of yours to work, I'll bet you can figure out a way to give us what we both want. When—if—you do, you know where to find me."

Under doctor's orders, Miranda had taken two weeks of vacation to rest and recuperate. She spent the first, sparring verbally with Trent. By comparison, the second was long and quiet and lonely. With Trent gone, she had to come to terms with how his departure affected her own future.

They were victims of circumstance. Each of them had their own goals, but a bizarre combination of loyalty and geography conspired to keep them from achieving their dreams together. Miranda didn't want a long-distance marriage, and Trent wouldn't settle for one. With him, it was all or nothing. He didn't think his demand was unreasonable.

She didn't either, really. True, he'd asked her to give up her job and move from her hometown. But in return, he was offering her the career opportunity of a lifetime. She'd have jumped at it, too, if she hadn't made the vow to Sam.

All week she wavered between fury—at herself for making the promise in the first place—and guilt, because she kept forgetting how much that promise had benefited her. By Friday, she longed to return to work just to shake the demons of indecision. She also couldn't wait to dress in real clothes again. Schlepping around in nightgowns and lying in bed didn't set well, doctors orders or no.

She had about decided to mutiny against them when the doorbell rang. "Sam," she exclaimed, delighted to have company, even if her appearance was a disaster.

"You look a damned sight better than you did in that hospital," he stated. "Glad to see some of what that sawbones told you got through."

"And I'm glad to see you," she told him sardonically. "This apartment, lovely as it is, resembles a cell after two weeks. I'm counting the hours until I get back to my job."

She heard Sam blow out a disgusted sigh as he followed her into the living room. "Your return to work is what I've come to talk about." Miranda settled herself on the couch, and he sat down in a chair across the room.

"What's so important about my job that it can't wait until Monday? Did something go wrong while I've been out?"

He flicked a hand in dismissal. "Nothing like that." He gazed around the room, paying attention to every detail. "One day at St. Luke's, Tom told me the doc said two weeks off was minimum, four would be better."

"Trent! He had no business telling you that, interfering. He isn't my keeper."

Sam's brows climbed. "My guess is he'd like to be."

Miranda bristled at his intimation. "Well, that would be pretty difficult with him in North Carolina and me here."

Before she caught on to what he was doing, Sam had her pouring out the whole story. Trent's permanent move and her misery over it. His proposal and her rejection of it. His offer of her own retreat and her refusal of it.

"Hang it, Miranda. What more do you want? If you don't beat all. Give you a good, strapping man who can provide you with *everything* any woman needs and what do you do with him? Send him packing." He scrabbled for his pipe.

"I had no choice."

"Hell! 'Course you did. You couldn've gone right along with him. Suppose that didn't occur to you?"

"More than once," she said softly. "I think . . . it's what . . ." No, she couldn't tell Sam what she wanted.

But as before, he didn't stop until he had all the details. "Don't you see? I *can't* go anywhere. I swore to work for you always, Sam. I'll never renege on that."

"What?" he bellowed. A barrage of creative curses colored the air. The match he'd just struck went flying. For once it landed in an ashtray. Sam didn't notice. "You turned down a marriage proposal and the chance to have your own business because of a promise you made to me when you were no more than a skinny kid looking for a break?"

"I meant it. I still do."

He tossed the pipe aside without ever getting it lighted. Then he came to sit beside her and took her hand. "Miranda, you've been like another daughter to me. I've had fourteen years of your loyalty, which is more than any employer has a right to ask. This shouldn't be necessary, but as of today, I'm releasing you from that promise and requesting your resignation."

Miranda's mouth dropped open. "But you— But, Sam—"

"No buts. I've worked hard, and I've been lucky. Still, I wouldn't trade success for Lucy and my kids. You made a promise in youthful exuberance, and you remembered it. Me, I never thought of it as etched in stone."

"This is too much to comprehend. What can I say?"

Sam's eyes bored into hers. "You love Tom Farraday?"

"With all my heart."

"Then that says it all."

"You know where to find me," Miranda fumed after stopping her rental car for the third time to ask directions. She'd been so ecstatic when she left Kansas City that morning, she could have flown to Charlotte without a plane. Driving into the mountains had brought her back to earth. If the last local was correct, the next left, then the second right would bring her to the place where there were a lot of "doins" going on.

Miranda had her own "doins" to take care of. She couldn't wait to see Trent. Driving slowly, she made the turns as directed and not only found the estate, but immediately spotted a workman who told her she'd find Trent at the main house.

Her eyes widened when she pulled around a curve. There it was, three stories and columns, like something out of the antebellum South. Miranda thought of Tara and wondered whimsically how it would feel to live like Scarlett. Then she saw him, standing at the top of a grand flight of stairs. The minute he spied the car, he started down the steps. Expecting her?

By the time she got out of the car, he was there to meet her with his I-could-eat-you-up grin. He kissed her then, long and deep and hard and hot, and it tasted better than anything had ever tasted in her life.

"You talked to Sam," was the first thing he said.

She was a little miffed that he'd figured it out and spoiled her surprise. "How did you guess?"

"Mandy, my love, you are the most practical woman I know. Sooner or later you had to see the most direct way of approaching the problem. I was betting on you. And Sam. What did he say?"

She laughed, liking the sound of *my love.* "Quite a lot, but you'll never hear me repeat words like that. The essence of all of it was that he couldn't believe I took the promise I made in youthful exuberance so seriously that I would let it rule my life. That as wonderful as I am, Callahan Associates can get along without me, whereas you, poor man, might not be able to."

"I couldn't have said it better. In fact, if Sam hadn't, I would have. Eventually. You may have thought I'd given up, Mandy, but I hadn't. Not by a long shot."

Knowing that filled her heart even fuller with

love, if that was possible. "Do you want to hear the rest, or just fill in the details on your own?"

"I want to hear everything. But first I want to show you something. Come this way."

They followed a path behind the house and through dense woods for about a quarter mile. At the split rail fence of a corral, Trent put two fingers to his mouth and whistled. A beautiful chestnut horse came galloping around the barn, head high, tail flying, flanks shining. Miranda's breath caught up in her throat. "How beautiful."

Trent held out his hand, and the horse came to nip at it. "That's my girl," he said, and a sugar cube materialized from his pocket. He stroked the mare's muzzle, and she whickered her approval. Then he took Miranda's hand and held it out.

"Lady Jane, this is Mandy. And she can ride you any time she wants, right?"

"Trent, you remembered. Oh, thank you." Fulfilling her childhood fantasy was such a touching, impossibly sweet gesture. How had she been so lucky to have found the one man who could and would do that for her? She clamped her eyes shut. "Rats. I never used to cry over anything." But she had cried gallons when she believed she'd lost Trent.

His arm wrapped around her, hugging tightly. "Well, get used to it. Lady Jane's just the beginning. There's a whole lot more where she came from. I'm not above resorting to bribery to keep you where I want you, which is just this close."

"But don't you see? That's not why I'm here, not for things. I've discovered that all I really want and need is to be with you, just this close."

Trent touched her lips with his. "That has to be the best news I've ever heard in my life."

"Better than hearing that I love you?"

"How about equally good? The difference is, now that I know you'll be with me, I will expect to be hearing the 'I love you' part real often."

"Count on it," Miranda said, feeling younger and happier than she could ever remember. What a revelation to learn that something that hadn't even made her goal list could bring her this much pleasure. "I love you!"

"And I love you, Mandy. More than you can imagine." Entwining their fingers, he turned her back toward the house. Her new home.

They climbed the steps to the porch, and Trent described the layout of the grounds, including where Miranda's retreat would be constructed. "As soon as you're settled, we can get started. We'll offer the contractor a hefty bonus for some fast work. See if we can't have it up and running by next summer."

"You didn't know, but this is my dream, transplanted about nine hundred miles to the east." She told him about the proposal she'd spent months working up. "I wanted to stop traveling so much, so I came up with the idea to bring people to me."

"Looks like we were thinking along the same lines." Trent's hands framed her face. "Mandy, I'm fully aware of all you're giving up for me. I'll do everything in my power to make sure you're not sorry."

Her hands covered his. "All my life I hungered to have money in the bank. A lot of it, so that if anything happened to me, I would never be forced to live the way my parents had to when I was growing up."

"I will see to it that you have money of your own, money nobody else can touch."

She shook her head. "It took hours of soul-searching for me to find out that the most important thing I need can't be bought. That's why I'm here."

Miranda gave him a smile of acceptance and promise. "That's another thing Sam said, as he left my apartment. Everything in life is a risk. And the best things come from taking the biggest risks."

Trent threw back his head and laughed. "Darlin', that first night when I saw your red silk kimono, I said to myself, 'That woman has an adventurous streak.'" He scooped her up into his arms and headed for the double doorway. "I made up my mind I was going to be the man to unleash it."

She speared her fingers into his hair and practiced a sultry drawl. "Darlin', you ain't seen nothin' yet. Adventurous is me packing a suitcase full of French perfume and silk undies . . . and no birth control pills."

Trent halted, looking stunned. "You mean . . ."

"Yep. Left 'em behind with the rest of my excess baggage."

THE EDITOR'S CORNER

LOVESWEPT sails into autumn with six marvelous romances featuring passionate, independent, and truly remarkable heroines. And you can be sure they each find the wonderful heroes they deserve. With temperatures starting to drop and daylight hours becoming shorter, there's no better time to cuddle up with a LOVESWEPT!

Leading our lineup for October is **IN ANNIE'S EYES** by Billie Green, LOVESWEPT #504. This emotionally powerful story is an example of the author's great skill in touching our hearts. Max Decatur was her first lover and her only love, and marrying him was Anne Seaton's dream come true. But in a moment of confusion and sorrow she left him, believing she stood in the way of his promising career. Now after eleven lonely years he's back in her life, and she's ready to face his anger and furious revenge. Max waited forever to hurt her, but seeing her again ignites long-buried desire. And suddenly nothing matters but rekindling the old flame of passion. . . . An absolute winner!

Linda Cajio comes up with the most unlikely couple—and plenty of laughter—in the utterly enchanting **NIGHT MUSIC**, LOVESWEPT #505. Hilary Rayburn can't turn down Devlin Kitteridge's scheme to bring her grandfather and his matchmaking grandmother together more than sixty years after a broken engagement—even if it means carrying on a charade as lovers. Dev and Hilary have nothing in common but their plan, yet she can't catch her breath when he draws her close and kisses her into sweet oblivion. Dev wants no part of this elegant social butterfly—until he succumbs to her sizzling warmth and vulnerable softness. You'll be thoroughly entertained as these two couples find their way to happy-ever-after.

Many of you might think of that wonderful song "Some Enchanted Evening" when you read the opening scenes of **TO GIVE A HEART WINGS** by Mary Kay McComas, LOVESWEPT #506. For it is across a crowded room that Colt McKinnon first spots Hannah Alexander, and right away he knows he must claim her. When he takes her hand to dance and feels her body cleave to his with electric satisfaction, this daredevil racer finally believes in love at first sight. But when the music stops Hannah escapes before he can discover her secret pain. How is she to know that he would track her down, determined to possess her and slay her dragons? There's no resisting Colt's strong arms and tender smile, and finally Hannah discovers how wonderful it is to fly on the wings of love.

A vacation in the Caribbean turns into an exciting and passionate adventure in **DATE WITH THE DEVIL** by Olivia Rupprecht, LOVESWEPT #507. When prim and proper Diedre Forsythe is marooned on an island in the Bermuda Triangle with only martial arts master Sterling Jakes for a companion, she thinks she's in trouble. She doesn't expect the thrill of Sterling's survival training or his spellbinding seduction. Finally she throws caution to the wind and surrenders to the risky promise of his intimate caress. He's a man of secrets and shadows, but he's also her destiny, her soulmate. If they're ever rescued from their paradise, would her newfound courage be strong enough to hold him? This is a riveting story written with great sensuality.

The latest from Lori Copeland, **MELANCHOLY BABY**, LOVESWEPT #508, will have you sighing for its handsome hell-raiser of a hero. Bud Huntington was the best-looking boy in high school, and the wildest—but now the reckless rebel is the local doctor, and the most gorgeous man Teal Anderson has seen. She wants him as much as ever—and Bud knows it! He understands just how to tease the cool redhead, to stoke the flames of her long-suppressed desire with kisses that demand a lifetime commitment. Teal shook off the dust of her small Missouri hometown for the excitement of a big city years ago, but circumstances forced her to return, and now in Bud's arms she knows she'll never be a melancholy baby again. You'll be enthralled with the way these two confront and solve their problems.

There can't be a more appropriate title than **DANGEROUS PROPOSITION** for Judy Gill's next LOVESWEPT, #509. It's bad enough that widow Liss Tremayne has to drive through a blizzard to get to the cattle ranch she's recently inherited, but she knows when she gets there she'll be sharing the place with a man who doesn't want her around. Still, Liss will dare anything to provide a good life for her two young sons. Kirk Allbright has his own reasons for wishing Liss hasn't invaded his sanctuary: the feminine scent of her hair, the silky feel of her skin, the sensual glow in her dark eyes—all are perilous to a cowboy who finds it hard to trust anyone. But the cold ache in their hearts melts as warm winter nights begin to work their magic. . . . You'll relish every moment in this touching love story.

FANFARE presents four truly spectacular books next month! Don't miss out on **RENDEZVOUS**, the new and fabulous historical novel by bestselling author Amanda Quick: **MIRACLE,** an unforgettable contemporary story of love and the collision of two worlds, from critically acclaimed Deborah Smith: **CIRCLE OF PEARLS,** a thrilling historical by immensely talented Rosalind Laker; and **FOREVER,** by Theresa Weir, a heart-grabbing contemporary romance.

Happy reading!

With warmest wishes,

Nita Taublib

Nita Taublib
Associate Publisher/LOVESWEPT
Publishing Associate/FANFARE

FANFARE SPECIAL OFFER

Be one of the first 100 people to collect 6 FANFARE logos (marked "special offer") and send them in with the completed coupon below. We'll send the first 50 people an autographed copy of Fayrene Preston's THE SWANSEA DESTINY, on sale in September! The second 50 people will receive an autographed copy of Deborah Smith's MIRACLE, on sale in October!

The FANFARE logos you need to collect are in the back of LOVESWEPT books #498 through #503. There is one FANFARE logo in the back of each book.

For a chance to receive an autographed copy of THE SWANSEA DESTINY or MIRACLE, fill in the coupon below (no photocopies or facsimiles allowed), cut it out and send it along with the 6 logos to:

FANFARE Special Offer
Department CK
Bantam Books
666 Fifth Avenue
New York, New York 10103

Here's my coupon and my 6 logos! If I am one of the first 50 people whose coupon you receive, please send me an autographed copy of THE SWANSEA DESTINY. If I am one of the second 50 people whose coupon you receive, please send me an autographed copy of MIRACLE.

Name _____

Address _____

City/State/Zip _____

Offer open only to residents of the United States, Puerto Rico and Canada. Void where prohibited, taxed or restricted. Allow 6-8 weeks after receipt of coupon for delivery. Bantam Books is not responsible for lost, incomplete or misdirected coupons. If your coupon and logos are not among the first 100 received, we will not be able to send you an autographed copy of either MIRACLE or THE SWANSEA DESTINY. Offer expires September 30, 1991.

Bantam Books   SW 9 - 10/91

A man and a woman who couldn't have been more different — all it took to bring them together was a...

Miracle
by
Deborah Smith

An unforgettable story of love and the collision of two worlds. From a shanty in the Georgia hills to a television studio in L.A., from the heat and dust of Africa to glittering Paris nights — with warm, humorous, passionate characters, MIRACLE weaves a spell in which love may be improbable but never impossible.

ON SALE IN OCTOBER 1991

The long-awaited prequel to the "SwanSea Place" LOVESWEPT series.

The SwanSea Destiny

by *Fayrene Preston*

Socialite Arabella Linden was a flamboyant as she was beautiful. When she walked into the ballroom at SwanSea Place leading two snow-white peacocks, Jake Deverell knew the woman was worthy prey. . . . And at the stroke of midnight as the twenties roared into the new year 1929, Jake set out to capture the lovely Arabella, and quickly found he was no longer a man on the prowl — but a man ensnared.

ON SALE IN SEPTEMBER 1991

 THE SYMBOL OF GREAT WOMEN'S FICTION FROM BANTAM
Ask for these titles at your favorite bookstore.

AN 360 - 10/91

THE LATEST IN BOOKS
AND AUDIO CASSETTES

Paperbacks

☐	28671	**NOBODY'S FAULT** Nancy Holmes	$5.95
☐	28412	**A SEASON OF SWANS** Celeste De Blasis	$5.95
☐	28354	**SEDUCTION** Amanda Quick	$4.50
☐	28594	**SURRENDER** Amanda Quick	$4.50
☐	28435	**WORLD OF DIFFERENCE** Leonia Blair	$5.95
☐	28416	**RIGHTFULLY MINE** Doris Mortman	$5.95
☐	27032	**FIRST BORN** Doris Mortman	$4.95
☐	27283	**BRAZEN VIRTUE** Nora Roberts	$4.50
☐	27891	**PEOPLE LIKE US** Dominick Dunne	$4.95
☐	27260	**WILD SWAN** Celeste De Blasis	$5.95
☐	25692	**SWAN'S CHANCE** Celeste De Blasis	$5.95
☐	27790	**A WOMAN OF SUBSTANCE** Barbara Taylor Bradford	$5.95

Audio

☐ **SEPTEMBER** by Rosamunde Pilcher
Performance by Lynn Redgrave
180 Mins. Double Cassette   45241-X $15.95

☐ **THE SHELL SEEKERS** by Rosamunde Pilcher
Performance by Lynn Redgrave
180 Mins. Double Cassette   48183-9 $14.95

☐ **COLD SASSY TREE** by Olive Ann Burns
Performance by Richard Thomas
180 Mins. Double Cassette   45166-9 $14.95

☐ **NOBODY'S FAULT** by Nancy Holmes
Performance by Geraldine James
180 Mins. Double Cassette   45250-9 $14.95

Bantam Books, Dept. FBS, 414 East Golf Road, Des Plaines, IL 60016

Please send me the items I have checked above. I am enclosing $_____
(please add $2.50 to cover postage and handling). Send check or money order,
no cash or C.O.D.s please. (Tape offer good in USA only.)

Mr/Ms _____

Address _____

City/State _____ Zip_____

Please allow four to six weeks for delivery.
Prices and availability subject to change without notice.

FBS–1/91